DRIED LEAF

DRIED LEAF

Shukno Pata

JHUMI

PARTRIDGE

To order additional copies of this book, contact
Partridge India
000 800 10062 62
orders.india@partridgepublishing.com

www.partridgepublishing.com/india

Contents

Acknowledgement

All my praises and thanks are to HIM without whom we are mere speck of dust. Against whose will, not the Sun will rise, nor the trees will bear leaves.

I bow to HIM, The Almighty, The Ever Merciful.

My family is my biggest support and I am nothing without them.

A special thanks to my Ma, who never lost her faith in me and my Bapi, who taught me to give words to my thoughts.

This piece of work is dedicated to my daughter, who wanted me to get it published.

'You care nothing of my pain,
      You take me to be dead.
But life still breathes in me,
      Even on that morbid fallen bed.

And yet, as a waste, you burn me
      Or dump me in a grave.
I still return back to life
      In an immortal shape.'

Any life, no matter how long and complex it may be........
is made up of a single moment......

The moment in which a man finds out......
once and for all.......who he is.......

by:
Jorge Luis Borges

Chapter 1

It was finally her time; the time she waited for since the break of the day, every day. The time that only belonged to her; the time when she could just be herself.

With everything been taken care of; all the rooms been tidily done; with all the curtains been nicely pulled and tied; the beds neatly made; the scattered mess cleaned up; the house having been dusted, mopped, arranged; the kitchen chores finally over with hot and spicy lunch waiting to be served, Mrs. Chatterjee, tending a satisfactory smile, proceeded towards the metal staircase that connected the upper part of the house to the terrace, for her afternoon tryst. Light-footedly, she began scaling up the solid ladder careful not to disturb the silence of the house with her echoing footsteps. She held one of her favorite books in one hand and carried a small radio-transistor in the other; her companions in her peace and quiet.

She was half way up, when the door-bell tweeted, pulsating against the unruffled walls, declaring domicile emptiness.

She stopped and waited. It chirped again and this time, not once but twice, announcing urgency. She looked into her wrist watch. It was fifteen minutes past one in the afternoon.

Too early for kids to return. Might be Arundhati.

Arundhati was her over-sized, middle-aged neighbour, who usually dropped in to enjoy a hot cup of tea with some mouth-watering gossips.

Disappointed at the possible prospect of detention from her loved sport, she dismounted the metal staircase, crossed the entire length of passage that was guarded by intricately designed metal banister on the right and reached the edge of the huge, beautifully carved marble stairwell that had its hand railings merging with the balustrade above, when the door-bell rang again. She descended the numerous flight of steps wondering where Kalki, her maid, was.

She paced the space in-between and pulled the heavy, finely sculpted mahogany door open by its copper handle.

To her utter dismay, the person standing outside had remotely no resemblance to her friend, Arundhati.

He was young, in his mid-twenties, of moderate height, fair complexioned; dressed in a pair of very common blue jeans and a black and grey stripped sweater. He had a straight nose, two deep set clear eyes and a pleasant grin; all in all, a boyish charm about his face that caught her.

He must be one of those!

Her eyes traced one big suitcase, one soft bag and a side bag hanging from his shoulder.

'Hello, madam.'

He spoke in a deep voice very much in contrast to his appearance.

'Yes?' She demanded.

'I am Shubham.'

He waited; his beady eyes surveying her face. She returned them back with a stone look, determined not to give in to the tactics of their breed; their efforts to develop spurious bonding to lure in the customers to meet their target.

'Shubham Sarkar, ma'am. And I'

'Don't mind. I don't need anything.' She cut him short to save time. 'Thank you.'

She pushed the door shut.

*   *   *

Confused and disheveled, he thought against ringing the bell again. Instead, he pulled his black, thick, small-screened cell phone out and dialed a number.

'Dada! She flung the door on my face!'

'Areey...Who flung the door on your face?'

A lazy voice replied in a constipated manner as if his mouth was blocked with something.

'Dada! This lady... the house... uncle sent me to. Some Chatterjee. I can't recall the name.'

He blabbered irritatingly.

'Ohho! Push the bell once more then. I am caught up with something really important!'

It barked from the other side before sleeping into silence.

Important! What am I here for. Picnic!

Shubham sighed out loud and pushed the bell harder, taking out his frustration on the lifeless button.

The door tweeted again and for a very long time.

Mrs. Chatterjee had already climbed up the main stairwell and had no intention to come down to attend to the nuisance those people had to offer.

'Kalki! Kalki!'

She called out for her maid instead.

A young lady in an ordinary cotton sari ran out from under the stairs.

'Ask him to go. Tell him not to disturb me again. Alright?'

Instructing her maid, Mrs. Chatterjee marched up to vanish in the upper part of the house.

The door creaked for the second time. Shubham pasted the plastic smile on his face once more to confront the lady again.

But his smile froze half-way. The lady who peeped out was distinguishingly different and distinctly unpleasant.

'Didi asked not to disturb her.'

She woofed as soon as she saw him without providing him with a chance. She turned to retreat when suddenly she swirled back.

'Or else she'll call the police!'

Raising her brows and pointing a finger, she warned him and slammed the door close after making her point.

'Dada. I am leaving!'

He yelled into his mobile.

'Leaving? - Hmm-Where?'

The same preoccupied voice answered, irritating him.

'I cannot ring the bell again. She threatened to call the cops!'

It was winter. But the Sun was bright. He had been waiting outside for almost fifteen minutes. The air was cool yet he was hot; annoyed.

'Wait! Wait!'

His guide on the other side was talking clearly for the first time.

'There must be some miss-understanding. Hold on for a second. I'll get back in five minutes.'

The line went dead again leaving an agitated Shubham alone at an unknown, unwelcoming doorstep.

*   *   *

Mrs. Chatterjee was lost deep in the lanes of British Calcutta during the early part of the century, when Kalki came running to the terrace.

'Didi, sir is on the phone. He wants to talk to you now!'

Without wasting another minute, Mrs. Chatterjee rushed down to her room to pick the receiver that was placed upside down from the telephone on the side table by her bed.

'Mahua, I suppose there is a man at the door.' Came in a commanding voice. 'Some Shubham Sarkar?'

'Yes.' She replied irresolutely.

'Let him in and get the guest room ready. He would be staying with us for a while.'

Before she could say or ask anything, the phone hung up. Helplessly, she replaced the receiver.

'Kalki! Get the guest room ready. We have a guest!'

*   *   *

The door unbolted for the third time. Shubham and Mrs. Chatterjee faced each other once again, but the situation had shifted.

Mrs. Chatterjee, in her light blue printed georgette sari, her hair tied in a neat bun on her nape, with a distinct mark of vermillion on her forehead and wearing a smile, stepped aside to let a very tired, tousled Shubham inside.

'I am really sorry. I wasn't informed.'

Awkward and apologetic, she held the door to let him drag his belongings along.

He whistled a sigh of relief to be in. Straightening his back, he looked around. The house appealed to him at once. It reflected the fineness of a professional hand.

A serpentine staircase just in front connected the lower house to the upper one. The common high roof of the stylish duplex was well decorated with crafty false ceiling and fashionable lights. The staircase divided the lower house into two halves. The left hand side of the hall contained a big majestically carved Rosewood dining table with chairs neatly tucked underneath, on the checker board marble floor. The sitting area was lavishly done with a jumbo black leather sofa-set; floor, laced with carpets.

A tall wall-mounted glass case with shelves and plaques laden with china, bronze and silver artifacts, was shining under the rays that filtered through the full length, delicately curtained windows.

On the right side, were three doors, two closed; one open. It was from that room that the lady of the house emerged.

'Your room is ready.'

She forced a smile.

'Thank you!'

He nodded in a dry manner.

Pulling his heavy luggage along, he staggered towards the directed room when she called out to him from behind.

'When would you like to have your lunch? I'll get it ready by then.'

'Don't bother. Please... I am done with my lunch. In fact, I'll go out now. Need to meet someone.'

'Ok.'

With no further exchange of words, both retired to the privacy of their worlds; Mrs. Chatterjee went up to her bedroom while Shubham entered the new room which was to be his ephemeral abode for a few days now.

The room was spacious; well arranged, he observed, like the main hall. Making his suitcase to stand by one of the walls, he ransacked into his soft bag and pulled out a white towel and went into the bathroom to freshen up. He was starving and needed to go out foraging for food; a price for the lie he had uttered to a strange lady under an even stranger circumstance. He couldn't design a decent meal from a woman who had threatened him with cops just a few minutes previously.

Mrs. Chatterjee was relieved too. Having a stranger as a guest was not at all a privilege, especially when unexpected. She was pleased, he was going out.

*   *   *

The oscillating pendulum of the mega sized wall-clock gonged nine times attracting Mrs. Chatterjee's attention.

She was seated on the sofa, beside a broad-shouldered, heavily-built man in wheatish skin; thickly haired, with streaks of white at the temples. His legs were spread long in front proclaiming a good height.

'If it wasn't for my boss!'

Mrs. Chatterjee watched him mutter under his breath while scanning through the newspaper.

'Did he say when he is returning?'

He rambled making it barely audible for her.

'No.' She replied, 'And I didn't ask him.' She added.

'Never thought Mr. Bharadwaj was serious!'

His casual tone drew her upright.

She didn't respond. His 'matter-of-fact' attitude teased her temper. Let alone consulting her for consent, she was compelled to entertain an obtrude without prior notice. Her lips curled jeeringly at her imagination.

'It was a long day. I am off to bed.'

Yawing, Mr. Chatterjee folded the newspaper, stretched his limbs, twisted his body, and erected himself.

Iffy, she shot up along with him.

'And what about him?

'What about him!' He rejoined. 'Ask Gopida to handle him when he comes.'

'But Gopida isn't here!'

'What do you expect! I should wait for him?'

Throwing a severe look at her, he began mounting the steps. Words surged up to her throat but she held them. She was too tired for a tussle.

Gazing the clock with droopy eyes, she wished if Gopida was there to save her the embarrassment. How relaxing it would have been to stretch her legs on her warm bed instead of curling on the sofa. Folding her legs up, she closed her eyes leaning back; her mind occupied with nothing but slumber.

*　　*　　*

Before landing at the Chatterjee's door, Shubham had been staying with his friend Yash Bharadwaj (his guide online), son of Shashi Bharadwaj. Yash had a big family consisting of his parents, three siblings; an aged divorced aunt and a cousin brother who had come hunting for a good job after completing his MBA.

Bharadwaj family, originally hailing from the adjoining state had migrated two generations ago into Kolkata and now were amongst the innate members of the Bengali society in that area.

The two married sisters, residing in Mussoorie and Jaipur, had suddenly planned to pay their family a visit together, messing the situation up for Shubham, who until then had been their guest-of-honour, ever since his visit. The senior Bharadwaj, a great admirer of Niranjan Sarkar, taking it to be a lapse in his personal responsibility towards his guest, dictated his terms on his subordinate, Mr. Chatterjee, compelling him to arrange for Shubham's comfortable stay in his house henceforth.

As an extension to his exaggerated fondness for Shubham, he had invited him to dine with them as he celebrated family get-together with his daughters and grand children.

*　　*　　*

The stillness of the deserted hall was enhanced by the rhythmic ticking of the pendulum and regular breathings of Mrs. Chatterjee. It was late into the night when the symphony was interrupted by the tweeting of the door-bell. Dizzily, she dragged herself to answer the call.

Shubham walked inside.

The poor state of Mrs. Chatterjee's stricken face caused his eyes to flutter edgily and he promptly hastened towards his room, to take cover.

'Is this your usual time of return?'

She stopped him with a very thick tone.

Her annoyance pricked him. He wasn't in her custody, neither had he asked her to wait and rain concern; similar to those unexpected showers that does no good but brings life to a sudden halt, causing the stenching drains to overflow and flood the roads. He hated them.

'I was caught up!'

'And you didn't find it necessary to inform?'

'I am sorry!' He retaliated. He wasn't a school boy. 'I forgot! I'll take care next time.'

His temper was soaring and he didn't want to lash it out on a lady.

Just few days...

Caressing his untamed mind to settle, he turned to propel himself when she held him again.

'I'll get your food.'

Perplexed, Shubham stared at her as she vanished into the kitchen. That shower was definitely unfamiliar rather unforeseen; outlandish.

He had seldom been waited to be served that late by any living soul ever. It was abnormal; unnatural for him but he felt a pang of guilt creeping inside. He walked over to the kitchen where he found Mrs. Chatterjee arranging plates and bowls.

'Mrs. Chatterjee. You don't have to do this.'

The softness in his tone made her sleep-laden eyes to bat sluggishly and fix at him. It was for the first time since their meeting that he had spoken in a tone that matched his guise. He had a very good voice!

'I had an invitation. I am Sorry. I should have told you.'

Encouraged by her tender look, he stepped inside the well-lit, modernly-equipped, and moderately-spaced cookery.

'Please, don't trouble yourself.'

'That's ok.'

She smiled responding to his politeness.

Her smile washed away the weight built inside him. He stepped further in.

'I know. It must be very uncomfortable for you to serve a stranger. Believe me. Uncle! Yash's father!'

He saw a line of doubt on her face.

'Mr. Bharadwaj?'

He paused but only for a second as she recognized the name no sooner it was taken.

'I tried to explain. But he won't listen.'

He saw her thick eyes drawing thinner.

'I'll check into some hotel tomorrow.'

A sign of amusement began building up on her face. She seemed to be relishing his words.

It pinched him but faintly.

'So. Relax.' He forced an assuring smile in compliance with hers.

'You talk too much!'

Smiling, her wide open eyes danced, brandishing an admonishing look.

'Go to bed.'

She turned to restore the cutleries back in their places; her lips curved, stretching her smile while he walked out, head down, feeling like a school-boy; shunned and dismissed.

Chapter 2

The walls turned red. He looked around. He knew the place. His lungs battled for breath; his chest expanding to its ultimate stretchable limit. It was the same suffocating chamber. He began twisting and turning, gasping for air. Distinct rotten reek like that of a dead animal had started seeping in, filling his nose. He tried to stand. But failed. The cabin was fast shrinking into a tight cube, like a tomb, closing on him. Scratching the walls with his clawed hands, he fought to break free. But all in vain. The weight on his chest was crushing him and he knew if he couldn't manage to get out, he surely would die. He could sniff death, waiting patiently for him somewhere; invisible but evident. His heart sank; his mind thickened with fear. The red was growing brighter; bolder; darker. Crimson to black. The air stiffened with the stinking odor, killing his lungs. It felt as though emitting from him. It was now the time. Breathing violently, he shut his eyes tight.

This is not real....it is only a dream....come on....get up... get UP.............GET UP.......GET UP!!

He sprang up to sit on his bed. His head was spinning, rotating inside its cranium; his eyes struggling to adjust to the surrounding. It was bright, not red; sunlight filling in, washing every corner of the room. He could see himself;

could feel his skin. Neither did he find himself decaying nor could he smell the stench anymore. It was warm and fragrant; fresh whiff of live flowers floating in through the open window. Breathing heavy, he wiped the sweat off his forehead with the sleeves of his night-shirt. It was a new day.

*　　*　　*

'Did you sleep well!'

Mrs. Chatterjee asked noticing the puffs beneath his eyes.

'Yes.'

He lied. His head was splitting into half.

'Good morning!'

Pulling one of the chairs, he took his position by the grand dining table trying to be polite to the inmates of the house.

Before he could actually push himself down on to the chair, a hand stretched out towards him, holding him mid-way.

'Hi!'

He looked up.

'Myself, Avni.'

The mistress of that sweet, bubbly voice was a very pretty face. Smiling, he took her hand.

This sudden action received a strong side-glance from the man who sat next to her. Quick to notice, Shubham released the hand immediately.

Buttering his toast, he sneaked a shot at the man. He was big, commanding; his presence controlling the air. Next to him, on his left, was seated the girl; fair-faced with sharp features; she wore a cheerful disposition. On his right, was a young boy; most probably in his later teens. The roughness of his chubby cheeks marked his sprouting manhood contrasting the boyish smoothness of his features. Unlike his sister, he resembled his father, though required time to grow that giant.

'So, you are Niranjan Sarkar's son?'

Mr. Chatterjee broke the ice between them with his hoarse tone and tight face.

'Yes sir.'

'And what do you do? Make films like your father?'

Battling with the soft yellowish *luchi* (Bengali deep fried flour- bread) on his platter, he asked.

Comparison. Shubham hated it. Detested the way it caused him to feel inconspicuous.

'I am a photographer. A fine arts'

'So! You click photos!' Cutting him in between, Mr. Chatterjee raised his brows.

The note of mockery in his tone poked Shubham and his loose temper began skidding, watching the corners of his host's mouth twist.

'Yes sir! I click pictures!'

The strength of Shubham's tone attracted not only his interrogator but his wife too; her liquid, heavily lashed eyes shining curiously at him.

The round mark of vermillion on her forehead was red; deep like the walls in his dream. He looked away.

'I get it from Mr. Bharadwaj that you have a house here?' The voice had thickened more.

'Yes sir. Four lanes from here. At Sunflower Path.'

'That huge red-bricked, single storey one? Next to Justice P.K.Sharma's house?'

'Yes.'

'Why then you not stay there?'

'It is under renovation.'

'Oh! that's alright. You can stay here.'

Mrs. Chatterjee interrupted remembering their conversation from the previous night.

'Why?'

The question came sharp from Mr. Chatterjee taking him completely by surprise. He didn't know how to weigh it. It was thrown open and obscure. He wasn't sure if it was directed to him or to Mrs. Chatterjee. He stared at her. She appeared as blank as an unlettered sheet.

'Why is it getting renovated?' He reiterated clearing the ambiguity.

'It is my property dealer's idea. He wanted to touch it up a bit before putting it on for sale. It is an old house!'

'Ah! It's a fortune!'

Sipping from his cup, he relished his hot tea with cool idea of crisp notes, Shubham realized.

'But why?' This time it was Mrs. Chatterjee, asking.

'Ma...it's an old house! Who wants to carry a crap? We too sold ours. This is so much better!'

Avni dropped in before Shubham could answer her mother.

'It's not a crap!' he rebuked. The way she used the word, hit him.

'I don't stay here, Mrs. Chatterjee.'

Taming his voice, he returned his attention to his hostess.

'Then you can let it on rent. After all it's your home. You must be having memories to'

'I don't need it.' He broke her in between.

He wanted to stop her from goggling for ideas to retain something that he so desperately wanted to get rid of.

'Mahua! Won't it be better, if we all mind our own businesses!'

Her face turned a deep shade of pink at her husband's comment and she dashed into the kitchen to hide her embarrassment.

The table was loaded with a variety of lovingly prepared, appetizing items, but he felt full. His hunger died. He needed to be careful next time.

*   *   *

It was one of those slack Sunday afternoons when body becomes flaccid and all one desires is to laze the day away on bed. With Yash busy playing a dutiful uncle to his half-a-dozen nieces and nephews, Shubham was left with nothing but to remain confined within the bounds of his room, dozing.

Lying flat on his belly, he was snoring, when the tranquil of his nap was penetrated by a long, loud, screech; a noise that shook him on his bed. Twisting and shifting a little, he waived it off, taking it to be a dreamy imagination, and pressed his eyes again. But, it shrieked another time; lasting, bursting into a cacophony, throwing him out of the bed.

Shaken, he jumped up and treaded out trailing the noise, determined to discover the source. He steered through the hall; climbed up the stairs and came to a halt realizing, he wasn't the only one in the quest.

Miss Chatterjee and her mother, both were peeping in through an ajar door. Being taller in the crowd, he peeked into from over them. It was Joy Chatterjee, on violin, catastrophically trying to get his nodes correct.

'Poor child! Has been trying so hard!' Moaned the mother.

'Ask him to stop! Please! Or we'll be deaf!' Complained the sister.

'Get him a teacher.' Murmured Shubham.

'He goes to classes.' Avni swung to face him. 'And he's the worst there!'

'But he is trying!' Mrs. Chatterjee protested.

The violin screamed once more in the most horrid manner Shubham had ever heard.

Without reckoning, he pushed into the room, to everyone's utter astonishment.

Seizing Joy, he straightened his back. Rounding him from behind, he supported Joy's hold on the fingerboard with one hand and gripped his other hand, guiding him with the stick.

Soon, the room filled with melodious strings of enchanting music; caressing, smoothening every twisted nerve; relaxing every stiffened fiber.

Shubham felt something unwind within as well, wheeling backwards; taking him away into a soft silkiness.

He could feel the warmth; smell the scent; see the buttery skin, glistened in sweat underneath,

Him!

He stopped abruptly. The room collapsed, vibrating into silence.

'Awesome!' Expelled Avni disrupting those floating, dwindling vibes. 'That was amazing!'

'Just had a few classes. That's all.'

Releasing Joy, he hastened out of the room; dark and despondent.

'You play well! Can you help him?'

'No. Mrs. Chatterjee, I am not well learned.' He forced an assuring smile, 'Was a disaster myself!'

'He has a test coming.'

'Mrs. Chatterjee, if I could, I surely would have.'

Convinced, she descended calmly.

But her peace couldn't pacify the roars reverberating inside his head. He had lied, deliberately; the reason being very different, buried deep in him. Neither had it to do anything with Joy's pathetic playing nor to his limited knowledge of music. It was something that had prevented him from playing ever since he had smashed his violin to pieces uncountable, years ago.

'Why did you choose to be a photographer?'

Avni's question jolted him to his senses.

'Because I like it.'

'What do you like about it? It must not be very lucrative. Unless you are exceptional!' She smirked. 'That's what Baba says.'

'Every profession needs extra sweat to outshine.' He smiled, 'I like it for...it is creative! Gives me freedom of expression!'

He pushed his smile harder while swearing under his breath. He had changed three jobs in last three years, all credited to that.

Freedom of expression!

'If it is creativity that you are anchored to, then why don't you make films, like your dad?'She shrugged her shoulders, 'Isn't it a bigger platform? And one, that yields better money?'

She rolled her eyes in a typical manner.

Wide, distinctly marked with kajal, her kohl eyes resembled those of her mother's, but were more expressive. And she spoke with them well, in collaboration.

'Do you dance?'

He wanted to derail her from that undesirable topic.

They were stepping down the stairwell together.

'No!' She turned to face him. 'Why?' She used them again.

He shook his head vaguely, shooing away the importance of her query. His purpose was served.

'Mister! I am not the timid- type, ok!' She said glaring at him. 'So keep your attitude to yourself! And I dance!' She continued in a self-assertive way. 'In parties. Well if you can call that a dance!' She concluded throwing a bewitching smile.

He was amused by her boldness. It was quite in contrast with her classical looks and was very appealing.

They reached the landing.

'What's your type, Violin-man?' She turned teasing him. 'Music. Romance. Romeo-type?'

'No!' He couldn't help but laugh. 'I love the outdoors.'

It was for this reason that he had chosen to pursue photography. It provided him with ample opportunities to stay outside; away further. Be unreachable.

'And parties?'

'Yeah!'

'Good! Now, there is this cool party on Saturday. I have a couple-pass.'

It had been just two days that they had met. He was dazed by her smart move.

'Ma has reservations against late nights. If you come along, then she might be a little less panicky. And if she is convinced, she will take care of Baba! I'll be spared from that long, irritating questionnaire! Who'll pick you? Who'll drop you? How will you manage so late at night? Who all were there? Huh!' She sighed irritatingly. 'You can be my alibi.'

Biting her lower lip, she waited for him to respond.

Shubham laughed at his foolishness. This girl was way smarter for him.

'They treat me as though I was born yesterday....Can't they see I am grown!'

'They are just being careful.'

'O yeah! You won't understand. No man ever does. Because no one asks you. Right?'

True. No one had ever been there to question, but it never pinched before as it did then. Reason, he could not understand for he disliked being questioned.

'Avni, look I have a prior engagement. Sorry...Not possible.'

Twisting her lips, she jerked her head in a disapproving way and walked away.

He wasn't there to mess around with the daughter of the house where he was just a guest for a few days; his instincts forbade him any association that might cost him more than he was willing to pay.

*   *   *

With the mercury column falling every day, the ferocity of
the Sun seemed to subside, blessing the days with warmth
while the cool breeze from the Bay induced freshness into
everything and everyone around.

But Mrs. Chatterjee was far from being fresh; she was
dark, gloomy, sitting alone in her room, tensed.

The main door to the hall creaked, followed by few
storming footsteps flying up. Her heart stopped beating.

'Mahua! Mahua!'

The bellowing shook the house.

Collecting herself together, she leaped out of her room.
The door to Joy's room was wide open and Avni was
standing by the door blocking the view. She knew he was
in there. She ran.

'You dumb! Good for nothing!'

He was fuming; face, red; eyes, protruding out; brows,
constricted to form a line.

'Do you even realize how I felt when that meek, non-
existent Sanyal came into my cabin carrying that bloody
box of sweets!'

He was shaking in rage.

She pushed into the room and stood in between her son
and her husband.

'He tried!'

She protested defending her son both with her words
and her body. She was afraid, her husband might hit her son.

'He failed!' He growled. 'And had let me down!'

He marched the room up and down like an animal on
prowl.

'No more violin for him! Do you get me? No more!'

Staring fiercely, he stomped out of the room without reading the malicious tint of rancor building in his son's eyes.

But it did not escape Mrs. Chatterjee's notice. It alarmed her.

'This all is your fault!'

Began Avni, no sooner had her father left to enhance Mrs. Chatterjee's distress. She gaped at her in dismay.

'You forced him into this, Ma!'

'I asked him! And he consented.'

'This idiot cannot even tie his shoe-laces properly. And you asked him for his consent! Give me a break! I'll tell you what it is all about!' She stepped in towering at her. 'You want to scale up the ladder, to come at par with your Kitty friends, using your kids!'

Mrs. Chatterjee listened in horror.

'Don't you Ma?'

'No!' I can never think of using you or Joy for'

'You can never use me!' She condoned. 'I am not your toy. I have my own mind. I am not like him. Fool!'

'Avni!' Mrs. Chatterjee lost her temper. 'How could you talk like that about your own brother!'

She was disturbed to find such lack of compassion in her daughter. That wasn't what she had been slogging for. All her painstaking endeavors would be meaningless if she was unable to device warmth in the most auspicious of all relations; between siblings. They were to look after each other when she won't be there anymore to care for them.

'Sorry, Ma!'

Sliding pitch of Avni's voice brought some solace to her mind.

'But I think he should care only about his grades. They are not good either. Baba will definitely kill him!'

*   *   *

Shubham had a long day. Most part of it was spent with Shyamal, his agent from the property dealer's office, discussing and discerning ways to scale down the cost of renovation; pacing the narrow, dirty lanes of the open market, searching and selecting paints and other materials to cover the newly scraped, peeled and re-mended walls and ceilings. A kind of work he was not at all used to but needed to look into due to circumstance.

By afternoon, he was free and decided to spend some time with Yash as both of them didn't get much time since his departure from the other's house. His plan didn't go well as Yash was stuck with his lady boss whom he found very difficult to handle.

In his place, Shubham had to take all the children to the movie that their uncle had promised for the sake of friendship; albeit, spending two and a half hours inside a close, dark room with six mini-monsters to cater to, was not at all the kind of leisure he was looking forward to.

He managed to return to the Chatterjee abode by eight in the evening.

The table was laden with a hoard of delicious food, as usual and he was feverishly hungry.

Loading his plate with two pieces of fried spicy circles of brinjal, a spoonful of mixed vegetable curry, a piece of mustard coated fish and a generous helping of rice, he sat to pacify his grumbling stomach observing the unusual silence hovering in the air.

His eyes moved from one to the other on the table. Mr. Chatterjee was macerating his food with stiff jaws; his natural spree of dumping others with questions was missing. Maybe, it was his day off, he thought grinning inside.

Avni too appeared very low in sprit, concentrating only on her food, munching in haste. Joy was calm, as normal as he always was; nibbling. Shubham turned his head slightly to his left to glance at Mrs. Chatterjee.

She wasn't eating at all. Playing with her spoon, she appeared morose. Lost.

'Is everything alright, Mrs. Chatterjee?' Pushing down the bulbous inside with water, he asked.

'Hunn!' She responded, absent-mindedly. 'Oh!...Yes!'

He could read, she was lying. He saw it in her eyes. They were dull. He instantly shifted his vision towards Avni hoping for her to react.

Instead, Mr. Chatterjee's deep voice greeted him.

'How is your work going on?'

That was their fifth dinner together and none had completed without Mr. Chatterjee's enquires regarding the progress of the work in his house. Shubham smiled; a very smart move to keep reinforcing his alien existence and remind him well that he won't be tolerated in the house a minute more than required. He too wanted to leave as soon as possible, so it did not bother him much. None the less, Mrs. Chatterjee's dry face did pinch him.

'What happened to Mrs. Chatterjee?'
He asked Avni the next morning, when they were alone.
'Nothing! She is fine!'
'No. She was sad last night. Was very quiet this morning too!'
'Ohh! She is upset. Joy flunked his violin test. Baba was furious. That's all. Nothing more.'
Shrugging her shoulders, she went off.

Shubham bit his lips. He had lived through that kind of situation; knew the atrociousness of its effect.

The thick concrete partition separating the two rooms provided little barrier against the arguments that had kept him awake for endless nights. His father's raised voice and his mother's moaning, filtered through the wall making him anxious and restless. Though he could never fathom the problem, as his repeated requests had been affectionately put down by his mother, stating it as adult business.
'Not for kids to bug their heads with.'
But he noticed that her head had remained sadly occupied. He had hated his father for maligning her.

And, it was one such argument that caused his young world to fall apart.

'Mrs. Chatterjee.'
Shubham's voice made her to swirl backwards on her heels.

'Oh! It's you!'

Pressing one hand on her chest, she exclaimed.

She wasn't used to having anyone on the terrace in the afternoons.

'Kalki told me..I can find you here.'

He observed that a corner of the terrace was nicely turned into a cozy sitting area. It had two cane chairs, one small coffee table and a swing. The whole area was shaded with an adjustable umbrella to cover it from the Sun. The four frontiers of the terrace were lined with different varieties of potted plants, flowering and non-flowering. All in all, a comfortable place to hang out, enjoying the warm Sun and cool wind, on a sunny, bright winter afternoon.

'I wanted to have a word with you.'

'Yes.'

Dropping the book from her hand on the table, she sat on the swing, giving it a gentle push to move rhythmically with the blowing breeze. He noticed that the book she had put down was one of the Bengali classics written by Tagore, *'SHESHER KABITA'* (Farewell Song).

'Mrs. Chatterjee. I am really very sorry!'

'For what?'

'About Joy's violin test.'

'Oh! That's ok. He wasn't good!'

She looked away; her face washing against the flurry of air.

'If you want I can look for a good teacher. Home tuitions helps.'

'That won't be necessary. He isn't learning violin anymore.'

Her smile, incapable of hiding her grief.

A knot inside his stomach tightened. His helplessness against his own self had partly been responsible for the situation and he was finding it hard to swallow. Her disappointment tortured him.

'Shubham, Joy was never a brilliant child. Had been struggling with his grades. Never been appreciated.'

She paused long, recollecting crumbs from her memory. Since his early childhood, Joy had been weak, mentally; a cause for her husband's dissatisfaction, to whom definition of a man was, bold.

Shubham sat watching her, waiting for her to come out of the trance herself. He didn't want to disturb anything, neither her nor the air.

'I thought music might cause him to change. Make him gain confidence.'

She paused again calculating the consequence of her decision.

'I was wrong.' She pushed out a heavy breath. 'I have caused him a greater insult. I am worried!'

It was a damp evening. A kind of evening when one can smell the water in the air; can feel its weight on the skin.

Shubham's uneasiness was aggravated by her misty eyes shining against the dull twilight.

He had long stopped feeling vulnerable; had seasoned and inoculated his senses against infectious emotions. A quality, that had saved him from getting pricked, but had gained him very few mates; an utmost necessity in his field of work, where connections and associations spoke better than talent, mostly.

Chapter 3

Born to a pair of Bengali parents, Shubham's family was nothing like the typical Bengali families where the members are blessed with a host of relatives to crowd various occasions; to enrich celebrations; to exchange the spillage of over the top emotions. To excite life in totality.

He had grown up in a comparatively bigger house with scanty members; two male servants; two maids and his parents with zero interaction with any people from either of his parent's family. It had never failed to astonish him, especially when he compared his life with that of his friends'. He had spent most of the *pujas* with only the inmates of the house participating in the ceremonies; excluding his father.

He was a non-believer; an atheist, unlike his mother, who was a God-Fearing soul. He had seen her seeking more forgiveness than blessings.

To young Shubham, the contrast between his parents had been elusive. He had failed to understand the irony of life that forced two such distinct personalities to co-exist under the same roof. While his mother had spent her days pestering various Gods and Goddesses to accept her repentance, his father had drank the nights out with his friends, celebrating *puja* in his style.

The Chatterjees were a devotional family as well; he had gathered from the humming hymns that occasionally reached his ears in the mornings. Being a reluctant believer and a night-owl, he preferred his bed more in the mornings. Further, his dreams, the ones that had slipped off from the status of nightmares due to their repetitiveness, allowing him to train his brain to beat them, caused enough psychological fatigue that required him to draw his mornings a little longer, to replenish.

And it was that Saturday, Avni had been excited about.

Although she had not picked the topic up another time, he resolved to keep himself out and hence, planned a late night-out with Yash. With everything put together, he pulled himself out of bed a little before noon. At ten past one, he set out to find Mrs. Chatterjee. He did not want her to wait to serve him yet another night.

Marching the metal stairs up hastily in his blue denims, he spotted her on the swing. She was laid straight on it.

The glory of the Sun was partially veiled by the adamant clouds that had been patrolling the sky for last two days.

A soft Rabindra geeti floated from an old, small transistor. She rested motionless with her eyes muffled in her arms; unaware and asleep.

Scrapping his scalp for a way to wake her up, his eyes fell on a notebook on the table. It lay there open, clipped apart with a pen. He picked it up.

'*as I fall off like golden shower sparkling in the Sun, my heart cries out. I want to go back, stick back to where I came from. This is scaring. I have been free for the first time in my entire life; left alone to wander in the wide world all by myself after remaining glued and protected for so long. I look up at the tree and plead to him to take me back. But he doesn't care. He is preparing for new foliage; new leaves to serve him. I shiver not just in fright but due to the strong wind that flew me off, away from my roots. I realize. This is my only chance. I beg to the mighty wind.*

'*Oh! Wind! Don't you let me down, like all those who have done before,*

Like the tree that shed me off, when I was not so strong to hold.

Take me along with you to distant land and seas,

I wish to touch the sand, feel the air, dance with the humming bees.'

'How could you?'

As though struck by thunder, she leaped and snatched the notebook.

'But that was wonderful! Let me read!'

'No!'

Tucking it under her, she sat folded on it with a flaring nose; crimson spreading on her skin.

'You write!'

'No!'

Like an adamant child, she retorted in monosyllable, to his great amusement.

'I could never have possibly imagined. Of all people! You would be infected with the habit of sneaking into other's possessions,' she glared at him. 'You don't look like one!'

The words fell out with immense rapidity exposing her insecurity from behind the curtain of indignation.

'I am sorry if I offended you. But believe me Mrs. Chatterjee...you are good!' He smiled mischievously, 'I don't regret sneaking into your diary at all.'

Holding on to the sternness, she pulled the notebook from under her.

'How much have you read?' She demanded.

'Pretty some pages. And I am impressed!'

Biting into his lower lip, he pulled a thumb up at her, appreciating.

'Just words. My thoughts. Nothing impressive to boast about.'

Saying, she bent forward to place it on the table. No sooner had she dropped the diary back, he reached out for it. She tapped his hand.

'No!'

And jerked it way.

'Then get them printed! At least, I'll be able to read then. You won't let me touch it otherwise!'

His eyes twinkled teasingly at her.

'You talk too much!'

Securing her property in her hand, she walked to stand next to a stout rose shrub with white flowers, by the wall.

'You are secretive.' He followed her, with his hands tucked inside his pockets, assuring her no mischief, 'Just like my Ma!'

'Really?'

'Yeah. She sang beautifully. But would shy away when requested to sing in public.'

'Does she live with you?'

Surprised, Shubham stared at her, scrutinizing the genuineness of her supposed ignorance.

She couldn't be joking?

Mrs. Chatterjee returned his penetrating gaze with a soft, genuine look.

He relaxed.

'No. She died. Nine years ago.'

The blatant nature of his statement touched her. She withdrew, observing the twinkle resigning from his eyes.

'I am sorry.'

'That's alright! I am perfectly at terms with it.'

The day suddenly grew grey.

'Where did she hail from?'

'Some place called Banipur.'

'Banipur! Where in Banipur?'

Curious, Mrs. Chatterjee turned to face him entirely, squeezing her big eyes.

'I don't know. I have never been there. But she often said that her house was big and had a huge courtyard within, named 'Thakur Bari'.'

Mrs. Chatterjee's doe eyes widened in astonishment.

Shubham was a little taken aback by her exalted interest.

'What was her name?'

'Swarnali'

'Thakur? Swarnali Thakur....of Thakur Bari?'

'Yes!'

'You are Swarnali's son!'

'You knew my mother?'

'Yes.'

Her voice blew out as a loud audible whisper expressing shock, confusing Shubham.

The dark clouds grew wicked, bulleting huge droplets, attacking down at them. Untimely drizzles caused them to run inside.

'How did you know Ma?'

Wiping his face with his hands, he followed her as they clattered down the metal stairwell.

'She was my didi's companion. They were very close, like sisters.'

Mind travels faster than time. She wasn't where she physically was, rather was skidding swiftly into the bygone lanes of the yesteryears; of reckless laughters, of endless ventures into the lush paddy fields, of innocent pranks.

A pair of fair faces smiled at her; swept by two red, wet, swollen, rheumy eyes; a hollow stare of few helpless faces; replaced by the body, lying lifeless on bed, in a yellow sari.

She shut her eyes clearing her brain and entered her room.

'Where does your sister live now?'

Unaware of her psyche, Shubham called from behind.

'She doesn't live anywhere.' She stopped near the door and turned, 'She died.'

Her last two words fell like stones in water, sinking deep, leaving only ripples on the surface; undulations that tickles one to be in awe at what caused them.

Shubham too wanted to discern the meaning of her words, but decided to wait. She had walked inside her room in complete indifference; rather occupied. Instead, he announced his late coming and departed.

Mrs. Chatterjee didn't clearly absorb what Shubham had said before leaving.

Swarnali.

Her mind was taken by the name; one that had caused so many lives to change; so many destinies to alter; so many dreams to shatter.

Shubham is Swarnali's son.

Stroking the face of her dairy absentmindedly, she sat at the edge of her bed, reckoning.

*   *   *

After a couple of Yash's last minute drafting and editing, Shubham and Yash hit the road in his much loved car; a silver-grey, Maruti-800. It was passed on to him from his father, Mr. Bharadwaj, after using it for five continuous years, when he bought a bigger and an expensive four wheel drive.

But to Yash, it was his baby. In spite of being on road for that long, it was in excellent condition, not because of the brand that happened to be one of the most reliable and sought out one, but because Yash cared for it more than anything else. His only personal possession in a family that shared everything; from toothpicks to tissue papers.

'What's wrong? Why are you playing with that phone of yours?' Asked Yash, brushing off his shabby hair from his forehead and adjusting his spectacles.

They were in a roadside *dhaba* (eatery) at the outskirts of the city by N.H.6 enjoying crisp brown *aloo paratha* (potato stuffed flour bread) and *lassi* (butter milk).

'Nothing.'

Picking his cell, Shubham dialed again. The screen remained luminescent for sometime before dying off.

'Who is this you are being so impatient about?'

'Avni.'

'Ahha!' Taking a big bite of his *paratha*, Yash danced his eyes teasingly on him. 'So, young miss Chatterjee is disturbing you. Well. Good choice!'

'She isn't my choice. I am just being a little curious.'

The *lassi* was colder than the air around and it ran a shiver down his spine.

'Well.'...*burp*.....'It all starts with curiosity, isn't it?'

Shubham was fixated. If Yash's enquiry was naive or deliberate, he wasn't clear, but he was in no mood to carry the discussion further in that direction.

'Where is this Banipur?'

He needed to divert the course.

'Not far. Why?'

'How about going on for a drive there?'

'Ok. But why? What purpose do you have there?'

'It's my mother's birth place.'

'There! There! There! Love for lost relations spouting out!'

Shubham perfectly knew the reason backing Yash's sarcasm.

Yash had always been insisting upon reviving relations since the time their friendship had vented out his constricted mind-set regarding his genealogy.

His companion had even suggested him, on his arrival, to reach out to his people, which Shubham had discarded as useless.

This cynicism was on board and he required to device a way to disembark it, to sail the ship of their amity smoothly.

*   *   *

'When is Avni returning?'
'She said, she will be back before midnight.'
'Where is the other one?'
'Which other one?'
'Shubham?'
'He has gone out too.'
'Together?'

Watching the pair of crow-feet pulled on the either side of her husband's eyes, she searched into her brain trying to locate Shubham's statement. He had said he was going out but did not mention going out with Avni.

'No.'

She replied with conviction.

'Better keep an eye on him. I don't trust that one.'

He threw a warning look at her.

'Avni should stop all these foolishness of hers now. The Bhattacharjees are interested.'

'But she is young! Don't you think we should give her a little more time. She has not finished her course. She might not comply with it.'

'Mahua! He refuted, 'A good family, with that kind of reputation and social status, does not knock your door every day. Talk to her. She will not get a husband like Raktim. Gem!'

Mrs. Chatterjee sauntered the hall remembering her husband's smug face; it reflected as if Raktim was his own son. She sighed.

Raktim Bhattacharjee was definitely a gem. He was well brought-up, well-educated, smart; an established CA working with a reputed firm.

Mr. Chatterjee had rejected her plea to let Avni pursue her career before marrying her off; his case being put forward with argument that Bhattacharjees were wealthy and Raktim was their only heir.

Do people work only for money? Or, to get a good husband, should be a girl's only aspiration?

She glanced at the big clock on the wall. It was very late; way beyond midnight; long passed the timeline set for her to return. Avni needs to learn to value her words, she murmured while trying her number with the cordless for the third time.

*   *   *

'Shubham. Are you home already?'

His phone buzzed to life; Avni's voice filling his ears. He looked at the time. It was half past one in the morning.

'No...About to. Why?'

'Then don't enter. Wait till I come.'

Disconnecting the line, he pressed his lips thin in irritation realizing what awaited. She had overruled the time limit and needed him to save her skin.

Bidding Yash good bye, he settled next to the tall iron gate, alone, under the dim light from the street lamp nearby.

The lane was barren, deserted; glowing soft under the effect of showering beams from the antiquely designed lamp posts with silhouette of houses lurking along the either side. A dog wailed somewhere at the distance. He was ill at ease.

He distasted a scenario of that kind; it caused his stomach to twist and churn, forcing his mind to that weird thought of a demon hiding in the dark; ready to pounce.

'Shubham. Come, let's go in. And be with me,' she ordered. 'Please!' She added later.

The greasiness of her sugary voice was no comfort to him.

It was not in him to take instructions easily. He wanted to give a piece of his mind to her, but he didn't. He listened. He could have rejected and walked away. Instead, he yoked himself with her. All for that lady who had known his mother; had not poked into his wound for cheap entertainment.

Avni dialed a number on her cell phone.

Mrs. Chatterjee lightly pushed the door close to avoid waking Mr. Chatterjee up, after sliding them in. Then she turned to face her daughter, who started even before being asked.

'Ma.. we were about to leave on time but got caught up by friends. And...I thought it was ok to stay a little longer. After all I wasn't alone.' She moved close to him and squeezed his arm, smilingly. 'He was there to take care of me.'

A puzzled Mrs. Chatterjee turned her squinted, inquiring eyes from her daughter to him. He lowered his head to avoid her gaze.

'I am tired! My ankles are aching....Can't stand for a second!'

Avni moved forward and dropped a peck on her mother's cheek.

'Good Night!'

With her shoes in hand, swaying from side to side gleefully, she danced up the stairs, humming happy tune, leaving behind a suspicious mother and agitated Shubham.

'Good Night Mrs. Chatterjee!'

Shubham departed.

Alone in the emptiness of the hall, she was left perturbed; upset. For some unknown reason, she had immense faith on Shubham; nevertheless irrational, she knew.

Apart from his identity and few meaningless afternoons that they had spent together, he was a stranger. She knew nothing about him. But she had no rights to complain about him when her own daughter had not cared to mention it to her; had played with her trust.

She needed to talk to Avni.

Or else it might all end in a nasty way, like before.

Chapter 4

'When did you get back last night, Avni?'

Mr. Chatterjee's firm tone threw her off and she bit her lip.

Shubham gawked at her waiting to hear what she had to offer her father.

'After one, Baba.'

Pulling a face as innocent as a child, Avni cooed to her father.

'Why so late?'

Mr. Chatterjee had returned from his Sunday golf session and was enjoying tea in the garden where he had summoned his daughter for a talk. Mrs. Chatterjee had laid the table with refreshments and got busy attending to her plants. That enquiry put her on guard. She dropped the water-can and moved towards her daughter to caution her. She wanted to hold it, deal with it at her level before presenting it to her husband, in private; not the least in Shubham's presence.

But the effect of Mr. Chatterjee's squeezed brows and tight voice were much too overriding than Mrs. Chatterjee's non-verbal warnings to her daughter.

Avni spilled it out.

She presented her crafted story from the night before with as much conviction as she could render, probably

41

hoping to salt away the building bitterness in her father's tongue. Instead, her narration turned him sour. He graced his wife with an acidic look which she embraced patiently; submitting to silence.

Shubham absorbed everything wordlessly, cursing himself. He had messed it up again for Mrs. Chatterjee.

Restless, he found her in the kitchen foraging into a purple, 210L refrigerator; digging out vegetables and leaves, probably, the menu for later meals.

He knocked to get her attention. She looked up, but didn't budge. The message was clear. She was very upset.

'Mrs. Chatterjee, I wish to confess something...if you have time.' He declared from the door.

'Yes.'

With her head inside the fridge, she was loading the tray next to her with eatables.

'I wasn't with Avni last night.'

'What? She lifted to stare at him, 'But she!'

'She lied.'

'And you helped her!'

'Yes.'

He stepped inside, searching for appropriate words to explain his point. He had helped Avni because he thought, his presence might dilute the pressure she was in; would provide her with some peace that her daughter wasn't alone. He wanted to be a consolation for her daughter's obdurate defiance to her instructions. But he realized that unintentionally, he had dragged her into deeper waters. Mr. Chatterjee had been more than upset. He had seen the icy glare whipping across, slashing her.

'I am sorry. I thought I was helping you. But I know, Mr. Chatterjee doesn't approve of my association with his daughter. So, I'll keep my distance. I never meant to trouble you.'

Stung by his revelation, she stood up. Handing the tray full of spinach, cabbage, capsicum and many other veggies to Kalki to wash, clean and chop, she chewed over Shubham's ability to judge and read the unspoken.

'That's not the case!'

She turned the other way to hide her discomfort. She wasn't prepared for this challenge.

She couldn't discard his thoughtfulness as nonsense and was under pressure to defend her husband's position. At the same time, she was ashamed of her daughter's shallow moral standard that lay disgracefully bare. She could neither apologize nor appreciate him. She preferred to concentrate on the cubed vegetables waiting to be cooked.

But deep within, she was relieved. He was more than trustworthy. He was dignified.

He knew, she was hurt. In his effort to wipe his hands off Avni, he had hurt her by laying open her daughter's immaturity.

'Mrs. Chatterjee.' He called from behind, 'Let's go to Banipur.' He said to cheer her.

She spun immediately gaping at him, aghast.

'Banipur?'

'Of course! It isn't far!'

'Do you really want to go there?'

Do you really want to go there?

He had heard it before.

It wasn't a question asked to assess the degree of willingness at all.

It was during *Durga puja* when he was thirteen, that his mother had expressed her wish to take him to Banipur, which his father had brutally dismissed.

'*My son will not set foot on that courtyard!*' He had pronounced breaking his mother into tears and bringing his young blood to boil.

'Don't you want to meet your people?'

Her reluctance, though not at all a match to his father's antagonism, was very abnormal; unnatural, especially for a conducive, encouraging woman of her kind to display remoteness towards her relations.

'I don't have anyone out there anymore. My people left that place long back.'

Her head was bustling and she found it difficult to focus. Shubham's approach to the subject was puzzling. And it cornered her.

'There is no point going there now, if you haven't been there before with your mother.'

'Why? Won't the people of 'Thakur Bari' acknowledge me without her?' He questioned her resistance.

'All I am saying is that...it may not be worth.'

She took her eyes off concluding the conversation.

Throwing the diced vegetables into the wok, she immersed herself into an opaque silence that barred him from percolating and he walked out deprived, in want of light; transparency.

Her evasiveness teased him; beguiled him to probe deeper. He wasn't ready to give up like his mother but grew resolved to find out the grounds beneath the preclusion that was so surprisingly common to both, his father and Mrs. Chatterjee; two people, not only poles apart in their character and approach towards life but were separated vastly by life itself; one was living while other had been dead, for three years now.

*   *   *

Yash was an easily pursuable man, at least to Shubham. He needed him because of his restricted knowledge of the neighbourhood. They hit the S.H -2 on Tuesday evening. The two and a half hours drive was smooth; the car cooing in the magical voice of Kishor Kumar from the bygone era, being played by the RJ of the newly launched FM channel; an additional accessory engineered into by Yash to enhance the luxury of his beloved vehicle.

On reaching, they checked into a guest house in the main market place. It was an old construction, made of wooden planks; scruffy and dilapidated, like one of those haunted houses from some erstwhile motion picture.

The lobby cum dining area had a small reception which consisted of a desk under the command of a manager, who appeared to have popped out of some comic book Shubham had read in his childhood. He had a thick moustache; black, covering most of his face. His dirty brown shirt had two buttons missing from the place where his belly had protruded out from the rest of his body.

A small television-set was elevated on the wall for everyone's view, which played an old Bengali film in black and white.

A tight, tapering wooden stairwell took them to the first floor. The narrow corridor was lit with bulbs hanging from the ceiling and was comparatively less crowded. Their room was at the far end. It was supposed to be a double room. But Shubham had never stayed in a double room which was slimmer than the singles he had known. It was constricted, with two beds lying on the either side of a table that was set by the only window in the room. A cupboard stood at one side of the main door at the foot of one bed and the other side had another door; the door to the bathroom cum toilet. This was apparently the best hotel close to the village they were to venture in. It was unbelievable that it was so close to one of the most famous tourist places in West Bengal.

'Sahib,' the teen aged boy, the bellboy of the guest house called out. 'You need to go down for food. No room service!'

'Oeye!' Yash yelled as the boy was preparing to leave, 'Can we get some tea?'

'No sahib. It is dinner time.' He was prompt and crisp. Must have been working since a small age. 'Sahib, down there in the bazaar, many tea stalls serve good tea. You can find one just opposite, in front.'

He left slamming the door, rocking the whole room. After freshening themselves, they went out into the marketplace to explore.

It was eleven in the morning, when they both commenced the journey towards their final destination; the *Thakur Bari*.

With the information they had gathered from the market the previous night, they took the first right exit from the main road and staggered onto a pebbled side road. As the car rattled on, cool, fresh air washed their faces, bathing them with the most picturesque beauty of mother nature, they had ever lived. The undulating wide, open lush-green meadows, touching the feet of the hillocks, mesmerized Shubham and tempted the photographer in him. He took out his camera and started clicking; capturing living moments with his lens.

'Two black bulls, each with a child on its back, tapping the street in style; a pair of young school girls on bicycles, smiling and waving at them; few naked boys clad in mud, fishing in a small pothole by the road; farmers tilling their lands; females washing clothes by the bank of the river that was flushing through; children hanging upside down from the branches of a big tamarind tree; a ghostly, time-torn yet elegant building, standing proud like a citadel from some history book; tall betel-nut trees with men raiding their crowns for nuts.'

'*Moshai*(Mister), which is the way to Thakur Bari?'
Confused with the network of narrow streets, Yash halted to take guidance from a man in white *dhoti* and *kurta*, standing by the road.
'Are you tourists?' He asked instead.
'We are from Kolkata. Need to go to Thakur Bari.' Yash said sticking his head out of the window, quenching his query.
'Yes. Yes. It's on my way. I'll take you there.'
Saying so, he started pulling the handle of the left rear door of the car, mercilessly. Yash couldn't stand to see his beloved being manhandled and unlocked it.

He dashed in without even the minimum courtesy of thanking.

'Let's go. Straight.'

Rather ordered as soon as he settled inside. Yash exchanged an eye with Shubham before steering the car forward. Meanwhile, their guide continued in the most unaffected manner.

'We have a lot of tourists to visit 'Raj Ghor', said he excitedly, expecting a similar response. 'You must have seen?'

'No.'

Shubham's reply drew his face long.

'Well, I am Shubham and this is Yash.'

He said extending his hand backwards with difficulty, which the man grabbed instantly.

'I am Jogon Rai. I work here in the Block Office.' He pronounced with self-importance. 'By the way, why do you want to go to Thakur Bari? Are you relatives to them?'

He smiled exposing his complete set of black teeth from incisors to molars.

'No. We have to see the family elder. Business.' Yash returned.

'Nilikanta Thakur?'

'Yes!'

Shubham read the uncertainty in his friend's voice while affirming Jogon. Yash had even thrown a quick glance at him in doubt. But, he was of no help; he was as lame on the matter as Yash.

'Very nice man.' Jogon shook his head appreciating, unaware of the flimsiness of their knowledge. 'Descendants of the royal family. The 'Raj Ghor'.'

'If I am not mistaken...you are talking about that old building we saw. One that looks like a palace?'

'Yes--Yes.'

The man satisfied Yash, the journalist.

'Once a very strong and influential family, upholding the torch of culture and tradition of this village. We all looked up to them,' he smiled sympathetically, 'But time has changed.'

'Why do you say so, Jogon Babu?' Shubham asked.

'Right.'

Shubham turned back to eye the man for meaning.

'Take right.' Jogon Rai signaled with his index finger. 'You see *Moshai,* not all the grapes in a bunch taste as sweet!' He said putting in a feeble effort to suppress the hint of mockery in his tone.

Shubham was prompt to read, so was Yash.

'And what is the sourness about?'

Shubham knew Yash was eyeing him. His tone was taut than usual.

'No..no *Moshai*. Nothing of the kind. Yes. We do not take them the way we did. But we still respect them. You are here for business and I should not spoil it.' He exposed his dirty dental set again. 'What good do we get from digging the dirt...except, wriggling worms crawling out from under!' He laughed lightly. 'You can stop here.'

The car breathed out a cloud of dust and died. Jogon Rai disembarked.

It was a junction of three pebbled roads. One headed towards right; one, to the left and one, straight ahead.

Jogon walked and bent over to talk to Yash.

'This way is my home.' He said pointing to the right. 'The third on the left side of the road. You take the left one.' He pointed to the opposite direction. 'It will take you

straight to Thakur Bari. And please....drop by for a cup
of tea!'

The car rocked once again on an uneven road which was
comparatively deserted. It was devoid of houses, rather had
thick plantation of mangoes and jackfruits speeding by, on
the either side of the road.

A huge, white, concrete house drew within view in a
short while. It stood alone with no other house in proximity,
proclaiming its dominance over the area.

Shubham sensed butterflies in his stomach for reasons
unknown.

The strong, magnificent iron gate, embedded inside the
cemented cartouche had no identification attached to it.
Most probably because it needed no plaque to tell its tale.

Both men dismounted after parking the car by the wall
and walked in.

It was everything his mother had told him. The house was
constructed surrounding the central courtyard that was
elevated by three continuous steps. The verandah of the
house was guarded by thick concrete balustrades on the
outer side facing the yard while was lined with doors on the
inner side.

It appeared busy; men, women, children moved in
and out of the rooms; ran about the yard. Few elderly
females were huddled together by the edge of the steps,
talking; spreading what looked like dried pieces of fruits or
vegetables, most probably to pickle them.

As both of them stood in the middle of the patio observing, a man, taller than Shubham, almost of Yash's height, neatly attired in maroon *kurta* and black *dhoti* treaded towards them with great liveliness. Densely haired, firmly built, sharp featured, older than both of them, he had an air of vanity about him.

'Yes. How can I help you?'

He spoke with silky-smooth politeness in a fine polished language.

'We came to see Nilikanta Thakur.' Announced Yash unsteadily.

'I am Nilikanta Thakur!'

The towering personality of the man unnerved Yash as he pulled the conversation on, exploiting his professional skills.

'Sir, we have come from Kolkata. Wanted to discuss something important with you.'

'Sure.'

He turned around, climbed the stairs back with same agility and vanished inside the house.

A little thick due to age, the man had striking resemblance to his mother. Shubham felt desolate; like that child who had been thrashed to the corner by his mates, for no fault of his own.

The man reappeared; this time with two helpers trotting behind. One carried two cane chairs and another, a chair and a small table. Arranging the furniture, they left like mute bonded laborers.

Signaling them to sit, he pulled his chair and sat.

'Now tell me....What business you have with me?'

He asked, delicately straightening the creases of his *kurta* by brushing it across his lap.

'*Cough!*' Yash cleared his throat. 'Sir, I am Yash Bharadwaj. I work for a magazine, and this is Shubham Sarkar!'

The very mention of the second name changed his expression. His well-practiced smile departed.

'Sarkar?' Squinting his eyes, he said, 'May I know your father's name, young man. You tickle my mind. You resemble a face!'

His tone, crisp, clear and firm.

Shubham took a deep breath.

'I am Swarnali Thakur's son....Shubham.'

The colour from the man's face drained. His body stiffened. Kicking his chair to make it topple backwards, he stood upright to his entire height towering on them.

'Take it back!'

He declared authoritatively to that poor, stooping man who was hurrying towards them carrying a tray with eatables. The man turned and frisked inside without any reaction.

The whole house came to a sudden stand-still; every eye gawking towards their direction. He stepped closer to Shubham with a constrained but severe intensity.

Both rose from their seats.

'How dare you set foot on my courtyard?' He gritted into Shubham's lobe. 'Haven't that bastard father of yours warned you? Didn't he tell you how I threw him out of this gate!'

His cold, hard, cruel eyes ejecting venom.

His vanity vanished and composure curbed by contempt.

'I have come here for my Ma!' Shubham retorted, 'She belonged to this house!'

Shubham had not expected great enthusiasm or excitement from the reunion.

No one from the family had ever knocked their door when his mother was living or even when she died. He couldn't recall any name or face to be present at her funeral or at her last rites. There had been no one to console him or tell him that he wasn't alone.

Yet he had come expecting a minimal courtesy; a general apathetic hospitality that of an ordinary interaction, common to any civilized society.

But what just occurred, was strange. Such insult was way beyond his imagination.

He was wild, furious; indignation trickling down his forehead as sweat.

'She never belonged to this place! We severed all our ties with her the day she sullied our good name. Have denounced her long back. What have you come seeking?'

'I didn't come seeking anything. I came to meet my mother's family!' Vexed, he screamed.

'Then Mr. Shubham Sarkar, you have arrived at a wrong address!' Nilikanta grumbled grinding his teeth, 'This is my house. Nilikanta Thakur's house! Bhabendra Nath Thakur's son's house! No Swarnali ever existed. If you will excuse me now.'

Disdainfully, he marched into the darkness of the house. The spell lifted. The mobility of the house restored. All returned to resume their suspended chores impressing as if nothing had happened; as tough they didn't exist.

Shubham remained rooted; his brain rattling inside his skull.

The picture of his mother's weathered face and lifeless body, in a ditch of blood, reeled, wringing his heart. He was enraged at their senile sensitivity; abashed at their lack of remorse with which they had shamelessly repudiated their blood, his mother.

'*Thakuma*(Grandmother)!' Yash called out shaking him out of his mental medley.

He was marching towards a lady; a very old lady, stooping under the weight of her age, from amongst the stupefied crowd, who had been eyeing Shubham intently, with a cocktail of grief, want and despair. Instead of responding to Yash's call, she began counting her steps towards the gate, throwing frequent backward glances at them.

Pulling Shubham along, Yash hurried out of the gate, trailing her path.

She was there, waiting in hiding, by the high wall, outside.

'*Thakuma!*'

Yash called out again. But she surpassed him and reached Shubham; her frail, skeletal hands caressing his chest.

'You are swarna's son!' Her voice was barely audible or readable.

'Yes!'

It escaped as a whisper.

Her loving touches were breaking him down and he swallowed the lump in his throat. He hated displaying weakness. He had faced it all alone; cried in seclusion but never shed a drop in public; never let it open for others to rub salt in his wounds.

'Have you known her?'

'Yes.' She sighed.

'Then please tell, what was all that about!'

She examined him with her squeezed beady eyes, those pulled inside the sockets; her wrinkled skin hung loose on to her bones developing furrows.

'Meet me after dark.'

Chapter 5

Shubham and Yash had a quiet lunch at a roadside eatery at the market place. It had a poster that read,

'MINAKSHI HOTEL--fish, meat, rice-- all available----EAT UNLIMITED.'

Although Yash tried few short topics for occasional discussions, Shubham preferred to remain aloof. Yash spent the later afternoon listening to local news and gathering gossips from the inhabitants.

Shubham watched him, feeling jealous. If only he had been able to pull the rein of his galloping desires, he would have been with the Chatterjees now; albeit not so encouraging but at least it wouldn't have been that worst. He enjoyed being with the lady of the house. She had an unique way to make him feel at home. She and her writings, interested him. He had spent some afternoons of the kind, reading and discussing different writers. It was with her that he had discovered his unexploited talent with the *Bangla* literature.

The reflection of Mrs. Chatterjee unwound him and he closed his eyes letting his mind to wallow in the luxury of her thoughts. He wanted to ease off the anxiety that the old lady had gifted him. He didn't know what lay in stock for him but whatever it held, he had a hunch, wasn't very pleasant.

The red fire ball drew closer to the horizon, painting steaks of purple on the murky blue sky. Each tree echoed with the chirping of birds in thousands, roosting back to their nests. It was dusk and the silver-grey car was parked by the big banyan tree that stood posted, guarding the junction where they had left Jogon Rai in the morning.

Shubham's eyes were glued to the lane that they had traveled just a few hours before; while Yash lay slump on the back seat with a *Bangla* newspaper spread on his face. His friend wasn't sleeping though, for he made occasional enquiries like if he could see her; what if someone followed her; why had she asked them to wait where there wasn't much space to park the car; how carelessly people drove bellowing dust; why couldn't they cross them slowly. Shubham understood his lamenting; the silver shining of his darling car was cloaked with a brown cover of earth.

Shortly, it was dark. Nothing was clearly visible. The fullness of the moon was overcast by shadowing clouds. Restless of waiting inside the car, both decided to stroll out. Soon, they realized their mistake.

A swarm of starving mosquitoes took them for feast. They began brandishing their limbs to wave them off. Nonetheless, the insects kept sucking.

It was when Shubham started wondering if she would ever come, that a hazy outline emerged from the dark and began inching forward towards them.

'Did you wait for long?' She talked in her drained voice.
'No.'
'Come with me. I stay nearby.'
'Can we take the car?' Yash jumped impatiently, scratching wild from the stings.

The engine vexed forward, taking them on a street that was designed with big dents at frequent intervals. The car rocked up and down; in and out of the dips and finally stopped in front of a small house that was unremarkable in the dark.

It was a half- wall cemented house with tin roof. She made them sit in a tiny room that had a bed and two wooden chairs for furniture and walked into the other. The room was dimly lit with a lantern placed in the middle on the floor; although, a light bulb and attached wire could be seen dangling from the cane ceiling. Mild commotion was heard from the other room suggesting the presence of many members.

She returned, followed by a young girl carrying two cups of tea that she placed on the bed in front of Yash who had made himself comfortable by stretching on it.

'Your mother called me '*Daima*'.' Cuddling the back of Shubham's hand with hers, she began, 'I was her nanny...A very beautiful child..Loved by all...Specially by her father.' She paused to breathe, 'She grew up to a lovely young girl... Both she and her friend Kakoli...were the heart of this place.. Their friendship appreciated by all.'

Shadows danced against the flickering flame of the lantern, on the naked wall. The time flew by, stealing the dirt away......

........*The black of the night was lightened; clear rays sparkling on the crystal water. The puddled, narrow, muddy lanes were lined with numbered houses, mostly with a skeleton of bamboo dressed with clay. The fields were not barren but had tall standing crops dancing with the breeze.........*

It was Banipur; twenty five years previously.

.......The underneath of a tall outstretched leafless Palash tree, the flame-of-the-forest, was orange with big, bright flowers, scattered, creating a bed. Two young girls, were merrily collecting them in the folds of their saris. Both fair lasses, free from care, engaged in fragile youthful endeavors, exhilarated the surroundings with mirth........

.......Walking hand in hand, they caught the eye of every passerby; their budding womanhood, irresistible to young and old, who teased them as they hurried away, shying........

'I often teased them saying that they should get married to the same man,' the monotonous whisper filled the background, 'They were inseparable!'

.........In a lavishly furnished, elegantly decorated hall, were present more than a dozen men, engrossed in deep discussion. A much younger Nilikanta was standing near an elder, a sturdy and honorable gentleman. They shared quite in common.

In an adjacent room, were gathered, a group of ladies of all age and size, around a brightly dressed young Swarnali, teasing and ragging her whilst she sat bashful with her face hidden in her palms, trying to hold her excitement.......

'Life does not remain same. It was soon time for them to taste the real world. Your mother got married to a very fine and well-to-do man from the nearby village.'

.....A palanquin with Swarnali inside, bolstered by four men on their shoulders, trailed by a hoard of people, carried her to

her new home. A plaintive Kakoli waved at her friend from the receding crowd with flooded eyes......

'Kakoli got engaged too.'

..... Draped in a beautiful yellow sari, Kakoli was presented to the guests along with refreshments. Her heavily lashed, brilliant eyes shined like gems as she dared to steal a look at the tall young man who was sitting in the center. Wheatish in colour, densely haired, with a sharp, pointed nose, he was relishing her with a pair of slow, lazy, curious, desiring eyes. A nervous smile quivered on to her lips......

'But all that happiness did not last long,' murmured the shaky voice, in her low tone, 'Swarnali's husband died in three months into marriage!'

'*Thakuma!* My father died three years previously, much later than Ma!

'The one who died wasn't your father.' She stopped and patted the back of his hand, with concern.

Something curled on Shubham's chest, like that of a snake; coiling, strengthening, preparing to strike.

Was that the ground, that caused them to remain detached, to spend nights in arguments. The reason his mother had been evoking each one of the deity, beseeching forgiveness; that they never had relatives. The reason behind Nilikanta's savagery.

She must have been another of Niranjan Sarkar's virile adventures that he couldn't cast off.

'The life of a widow....dreadful! With no love, no hope, it is a punishment. Casted off as a curse, thrown into the dungeon of eternal loneliness....life becomes a torture.....especially when someone is that young! Bodo Thakur.... her fahter, was devastated and brought her home.'

.....A ghostly figure in white, tucked at one corner of the room, sat folding her legs to her chest with tear-soaked face, denying plain food that her mother was trying to feed her. An equally mournful Kakoli approached and took the platter from the older woman and lifted a small amount of boiled rice to her friend's lips pleadingly. Swarnali responded and seized the bite.....

'Kakoli began spending whole of her days with her. This started easing Swarna. Bodo Thakur and his wife were delighted. In a short span of time.. your mother was beaming again. So...it was time for her to go back to her husband's house.'

The voice at the background crackled.

.....Carrying a tray with a tea-pot, two cups and saucers, Swarnali entered her father's bedroom. Placing it on the table next to the bed, she walked over and touched his feet. He blessed her patience and good life. She bowed to her mother next, who too prayed for her to be in peace with the life God had decided for her.....

'She went out with Kakoli.......And didn't return.'

Shubham sat quiet. He knew what happened next. He dreaded to ask. Rather prayed that she would stop.

'What a mayhem it was!...Bodo Thakur couldn't believe!....His wife took to bed....'

'She must have returned?' Yash's voice disturbed Shubham. He didn't want to know any further, 'Or was Nilikanta lying?'

'Oh yes!......Few months after,' she turned to Shubham, 'With your father. She came to announce their marriage and plead clemency and acceptance into the family.'

Shubham looked straight at Yash. He appeared somber and attentive; the way he had been at the time of his father's death. He sighed gratitude.

The coils disentangled. The snake inside slithered away without striking.

Thankfully, she was not one of his fleeting affairs.

'But it was too late by then....She had not just lost her father's affection but her mother too..'

......A bawling Swarnali was at her father's feet, begging for forgiveness. A cold Bodo Thakur stood rooted; unmoved. A furious Nilikanta pulled her aside mercilessly. Niranjan intervened. Nilikanta along with few other men lashed out physically at Niranjan. Swarnali ran to save her husband. Bodo Thakur stepped in and pulled Nilikanta inside the house signaling Swarnali and her husband to leave.....

'Foolish girl! How couldn't she fathom the vile consequences! Blasphemous! She had done what widows were not even allowed to dream! Had provided with a chance for everyone to point a finger at her family. Disgraceful!' Shubham saw a glint of fury in those anguish-stricken elfin eyes. 'Never saw her again! Just heard her news!'

The local dailies had refilled numerous cartridges over it for many days.

'HUSBAND TAKEN INTO CUSTODY AS THE MAIN SUSPECT.'

The wife of one of the upcoming directors of Tollywood was found smeared in blood in her own bedroom. Police is digging into it. She was discovered yesterday morning in her room with both her wrists slit. On the face, it looks like a suicide but investigation is on. Mr. Niranjan Sarkar, the husband of the deceased had stated that he was not at home. Police have questioned maids and other inmates of the house. A small boy, fifteen by age, is yet to be questioned. He is right now not responding. Appears to be in a state of shock. Following the footsteps of Satyajit Ray and Ritwik Ghatak, this film-maker has recently evoked appreciation for his off-beat topics in the line of Parallel Cinema. But what happened yesterday defines an undercurrent in the home front that needs serious brooding. Is the lust for poetic justice, depicted on screen, just a zeal to lure name and fame?.........So forth and so on.

'But she had always desired to come!'

'After all, bonds of blood, cannot be severed!' She smiled to draw grooves on her skinny cheeks. 'It is better that she never came! Wife's death had broken Bodo Thakur and soon he too was bed-ridden. Nilikanta took over everything'. She broke.

Squinting, she transferred her entire concentration on to Shubham.

'Well, I don't know if this is of any use to you....but this morning after you left, I heard him talking about a Will!' She looked at Shubham intensely. 'I am old but...I can read people. He wasn't his usual self!'

Shubham's eyes caught Yash. He was staring at him inquisitively.

'Oh! How dreary had all that been! Who had known the destiny! Had Bodo Thakur ever imagined that he was to witness such shame and loss because of the girl whom he had so adoringly raised? Had Swarnali ever contemplated that her quixotic antic would cause such atrocity? Had Kakoli ever known that helping her friend would cost her, her life!'

'What!' Yash jumped.

'She poisoned herself.'

'But why?'

'To survive Nilikanta's viciousness requires Gods to descend from the sky to shield! He had left no stone unturned to penalize her for helping his sister besmirch their respect. Threw the family out of the community. Got them declared outcast. Stopped their supplies. Caused them to suffer for every single morsel! Forced them to leave Banipur, forever.'

The room was cold and gloomy. The light from the lantern was growing thinner in the want of fuel. Shubham suddenly found it hard to tolerate and shuddered. Mrs. Chatterjee's sister had been dead because of his parents. No wonder, she was reluctant.

.....It was morning. The family was gathered to mull over something important. A shrill, penetrating scream resonated the air. Everybody ran to locate the cause. A female body,

wearing a yellow sari was lying on the bed. Face blanched; eyes out-stretched; lips, black and parted, she was oozing a mass of white foam from the sides of her mouth.....

'Silly girl! What was she thinking! She had overruled the norms of the society! Challenged the laws! Shook the foundation of the most prestigious family! She was bound to pay the price.'

The quavering voice resolved to rest.

'*Thakuma* mentioned a Will?'

Yash said from inside the pale yellow mosquito net, adjusting his pillow on his tiny bed.

The night was damp. The room smelled awful. Very rare to that time of the year, strong winds dashed on to the loose window panes, clattering them. The sound was disturbing. Shubham wanted quiet. He needed to swallow all that he had learned.

'I think Nilikanta deliberately kept your mother away. This Will has something to do with all this.' He paused only to continue. 'What do you say?'

'May be.' He wished his friend would stop prodding.

'Shubham. Are you listening!'

'Dada! Even if there is a Will, then I don't have it.'

'Then we need to find it!'

The excitement in Yash's voice reminded him of those childhood games he had played with his mother where he was to search out small treasures, that she would hide. During one such occasion, he got locked up in the store. He was later rescued unconscious. When he had come back to senses, he found his mother crying bitterly beside him while his father, ferociously furious, had been beating the room, reprimanding her.

'I am sorry...I was occupied and forgot about you....How could I be so careless.... I am not a good mother.' She had apologized folding her hands on her chest. She was pale; had looked sick.

Ever since, he hated close chambers. Preferred stairs to elevators, especially one without a lift-man.

'Let's go there tomorrow and'
'No! We are going back!'

He had had enough of Banipur. He wanted to return; go back to the security of his odd unhinged life; free and far from Nilikanta and his malice; from Kakoli and her harrowing doom; from the place and its poignancies.

Fortunately, Yash did not push any further. Rather, turned to face the wall and slept. Regular whistles of snore occupied the air within minutes. He too turned towards the wall; the pale yellow mosquito net brushing his face. He shut his eyes chasing his own train of thoughts.

His father's rigidity towards his mother's family could be justified now; yet wasn't enough to console him. His mother had been ripped apart from her family and his father had done absolutely nothing to heal the wound. He had been busy soaring the heights of success; fancying his lust for worldly glories, when she had bled in the want of an ordinary life.

He grew numb musing about the lampoon of life; one friend gave up her life to make the other one happy whilst, the other one in pursuit of her happiness, met her end in a similar fashion.

* * *

She was tired. It had been a very busy day. Stretching her legs on the bed, Mrs. Chatterjee wheeled back the events in her mind.

The Bhattacherjees had visited as a part of formal meeting to discuss the various aspects of the forth coming marriage. It wasn't the first time that they had met, but it was definitely different. They did not arrive as friend, but had been ballooning with the air of superiority that normally characterizes the upright nostrils of the groom's family.

Adding to it, was her husband's extreme stickiness to glue the two families together. She knew that his extravagant articulacy was guided by his desire for his daughter's goodwill, yet his fatherhood couldn't hold his lust for uplifted social status from leaking out; a craving that ran with his blood in his veins; that had been his driving force that pulled him from scrap to sky; from that deplorable, abject, downtrodden condition she had lived during the initial years of her marriage, with six members sharing two rooms of a small house, to that magnificent duplex that he had purchased four years ago and enlisted himself amongst the gilt-edged nobles of the locality.

'What are you thinking?' He asked blowing puffs of smoke after a long drag from his cigarette, 'I told you, I won't let them slip off my fingers,' shaking his feet on the bed merrily, he went on. 'Can't wait to see the neighbours nib their nails trying to figure how I hooked them when every damn house had been on the same goose chase!'

A light, soft laughter chortled out of Mrs. Chatterjee. It boosted him to smirk, expanding his chest by two inches more. Mrs. Chatterjee noticed but didn't react; allowed him the thrill of blowing his bugle of victory. She was plying a variety of other ideas.

Marriage isn't just about hooking someone; it is a symbiosis, where both the partners should support each other's individual growth while taking the relation forward, together. It should be complacent for both, for the relation to survive and prosper. Hope Avni understands.

'Can't we wait till she finishes her course? It's just three months to completion!' She urged.

'No!' Crushing the stub into the ash-tray, he snarled, 'She can continue later if she wants. Raktim won't object, I am sure. But delaying can be risky. Don't forget Mahua, we are the bride's party. We should be compliant.'

She chuckled again. How could she forget that. The bride's side must always be meek.

Her father had to reduce himself to his knees, to get one of his daughters off his shoulders.

'Where is that Shubham? We would need that room.'

'He said his house is almost done.'

She saved herself from answering the first part. She didn't want him to discover the tie that held two of them together. She and her sister had already reimbursed it with their lives. She didn't want Shubham to cartwheel everything back to start.

One for the other; Younger for the older; Mahua for Kakoli.
She lived the plight of those words yet again. Her head throbbed. She had to keep Shubham, a secret.
'Good!'
Switching the light off, he slid inside the blanket.

'Have you seen any of his father's films?'
'I don't have time to weep for others. I've heard, he was good. Dealt with socio-political issues.'
He covered his head and began snoring almost instantly.

Lying awake, she envied her husband. She was exhausted; wanted to sleep. But her restless mind refused to give in. In spite of her, it kept wondering about Shubham and his retrospective expedition to disentomb his past. In those few days, she had known him to be an introvert; an insecure and found it compelling to protect him from being marred.

Chapter 6

The tiny-clogged room went dark. He felt strange. He didn't remember switching the lights off.

Must be load-shedding.

He opened his mouth and called out to Yash. Surprising. He couldn't hear his voice. Clearing his throat, he tried again. Yet, nothing happened; no sound; not even a whisper escaped. His larynx was jammed. Fretful, he decided to shake his friend up for help. Strange. His solid body won't move.

A familiar strong stink started to fill in. Instantly he realized where he was. He was in his dream. He pulled himself together. He knew how to get out. Yet, his skilled psyche was unable to stop the walls from changing to red. He began panting. The air wasn't piping sufficiently into his lungs, no matter how powerfully he inhaled. He knew, he needed to force himself out, as always.

But, something was wrong! Where were the words? He wasn't able to locate them. His heart pounded violently against his ribs. Pinning his mind, he labored with all his strength to remember; but of no use. Those magical words refused to be trapped.

Horrified, he searched for an alternative exit. None could he see. Everything was red; just red. No doors, no walls, no outlets. All dissolved into space; vast, limitless, never ending, horribly red space. He knew, that was it.

My end.....The skulking demon has finally succeeded!

He closed his eyes in surrender.

A streak of white light penetrated in from somewhere. He raked the vestiges of his worn out, disoriented mind to identify the source.

A fairy!...A Goddess!...

The ghost drew nearer.

....Mrs. Chatterjee.

Without wasting, he jumped and wrapped himself around her. She accepted him in a warm embrace. Every other thing dispersed. The red disintegrated into a serene white. His body slackened at the feel of hers.

'Shubham! Shubham!'

A voice infiltrated into his brain as he nestled on her breasts. Annoyed, he strained his eyes to open. Two black beads swimming in a pair of pearly ponds hung over him. He lurched away.

'Shubham!' Yash yelled.

'Yeah!'

'Are you ok!'

'Yes. Why?' Wheezing, he responded adjusting his vision.

'You have been twisting and turning! Moaning! Did you have a bad dream?'

'May be. Not sure. Can't remember.'

He didn't want Yash to dig into the mushy mausoleum of his days of yore; wanted to keep him away from polluting that splendid amorphous rendezvous of his past and present, that he had just lived. He didn't want to let his friend lecture him on the alluring presence of Mrs. Chatterjee as his savior. He just desired to contain it within him; unspoiled and unmarked. It had been the first time ever since the advent of those notorious dreams, that he was feeling so tranquil; so complete.

'Come on! I don't want to live on leftovers!' Yash rightfully reminded.

Last night's dinner had been the worst food he had ever stuffed his stomach with. Late, as they had been while returning from *Thakuma's* house, their plates were dressed with what was left stuck on to the bottom of the utensils.

That memory changed his state of inertia, from rest to motion.

Shubham was in a great mood. The hot *Aloor Dom* (potato curry) with soft, puffy *puris* felt heavenly. On the top, he had woken up from his trance without an aching head. Eating in that open dining area, surrounded by noisy, un-groomed crowd, in that busy, bantam market place, felt orderly to him. The place wasn't that ominous anymore; he could see life all around, in all known forms.

Perched on the steps of the guest house, was a middle-aged man, portraying to be blind; honest or acting, he was not clear. Frayed in tatter, he was praying for *mazuma* (money) mercy to satisfy the grumblings of his deprived stomach. Shubham watched. A very common sight in Kolkata. Normally, the palpable fakeness of such people irritated him.

But there, as he relished the sweet *kheer* (rice porridge) melt in his mouth, he felt otherwise. After all, earning by playing beneath morality, had been a timeless fashion; ever-existing and everlasting. Easy and quick; everyone's choice.

Criticized only by those, who couldn't manage a chance for themselves.

And why not? Beggars were everywhere, to flush out the guilt.

Just requires a coin or two!

'It's not eight yet. Come. I don't want to miss him.' Yash said breaking in.

'I told you, I am not going there again!'

'Arey! I have enjoyed enough of your uncle's warmth! I want to see Jogon Rai.'

'What! Why?'

'Yes. Have some business with him. And he owes me that forced lift in my car.'

Shubham was still to gauge the bottom of his friend's intellect when Yash fisted two *puris* from the basket, crossed the entire length of the dining area and dropped them in the beggar's bowl.

Displeasure was written all over his face, when the man's expert fingers felt the soft puffs instead of hard pennies. But he didn't let the rope loose. Asking for prosperity and bounty from Almighty, he pulled the drama with practiced proficiency.

The show must go on!

Shubham smiled as he followed his friend to the first floor.

Instead of taking the left, the car steered to the right and came to stop in front of the third house on the left. This side was very different from the other, he had visited the previous day. The houses, mostly ordinary, were arranged in the most irregular fashion as compared to the stately unity of the lone house on the other part.

'Is this Jogon Rai's house?'

'Yes....' A small girl sang at the door, jiggling her doll.

'Can you please call him?'

Yash requested as the girl got busy singing a lullaby while combing her doll's thread hair.

'Baba!....Baba!'

She shouted from the door. She refused to either look up or shift from the place. Just kept repeating the lines in her juvenile, amateur voice.

'Ghum parani mashi pishi...

Moder bari esho...

Khat nai, palong nai...

Chokh pete bosho...

Bata bhora paan debo...

Gaal bhore kheyo...

Khokar chokhe ghum nai...

Ghum diye jeyo...'

(Aunties who put us to sleep...

Come to our house....

There's no bed, no mattress......

Sit on the eyes....

We'll give you a plate full of betel leaves...

Eat mouthful......

There's no sleep in my baby's eyes....

Lend him some sleep before you go........)

And peacefully, he would sleep. But as he grew up and was shifted to his own bedroom, he yearned for those jocund moments. Spread out on the bed, he would let his mother's honey voice melt him into a world of golden leaves and silver flowers; of fairies and angels. A fairy to gift blissful dreams; an angel to grant restful nights.

Like her.

'Ohho! Yash Babu! Welcome.' Jogon Rai wished them cheerfully inviting them inside.

'Hope we didn't disturb you.'

'Not at all! I would have missed you if you were a little late. I need to go to the PHC today.' Taking pride in explaining his work, he hushed his daughter and urged her to go in, 'Moina, ask your Ma to get something. We have guests from Kolkata.'

Shubham didn't like it quite much. He was enjoying her singing.

'Jogon Babu, I work as the sub-editor to the magazine 'The Onset'.' Yash pulled out a card and handed it to Jogon who accepted it graciously. 'How about a little interview?'

'Interview!' Jogon repeated flabbergasted.

'Jogon Babu, this place has immense potential. But what I have seen, I feel this place has been overshadowed by the much famous neighbourhood. It has its own story to tell.'

'Oh! Yes. Have you seen 'Raj Ghor'?'

Jogon seemed stuck to the place, to Shubham.

'We will, today. But before, we would like to get some knowledge about the place.'

Jogon smirked. Yash's professionalism captured him.

'Actually, you see, Raj Ghor was the winter palace built by Raja Rudra Ray Choudhury from the 'Ray Choudhury' family of *Jamindars* (landlords). It came to power by the 18th century, most probably. Their original palace still exists in the northern part of Bengal.'

He paused as a lady walked in, withdrawn in her sari and placed a platter full of freshly prepared *pati-sheptas* (cream rolls) in front.

'Please.'

Jogon insisted his guests to taste. Shubham and Yash took one each.

'Except for a few original tribes, most are the descendants of the people engaged by the Raja in various services for the Royal family like artisans, peasants, craftsmen, soldiers et cetra...Those deployed to keep the place within grip. With the plateau on one side and rich alluvial soil on the other, cut through by the vast river, the place held huge agricultural potential, which was the family's biggest interest, apart from its natural beauty.'

'So, how long did the 'Ray Choudhurys' rule?'

Yash asked battling to remove sticky bits of juicy *pati-shepta* from his teeth with his tongue.

'Not long. You see...They too fell to the British like the rest. Submitted to their alliance to save themselves!'

'Well, yesterday, you mentioned that the Thakur family had Royal links?'

Shubham turned a sharp eye on to his friend in disbelief.

'Well yes. That is the common belief out here. Though I cannot pin the link. Some say that maybe a woman or two at some point of time had been married with the Thakurs, who then served as priests to the Royal Family. But one thing is for sure. The Thakurs had been greatly patronized by the Royal family. They were and still are, the biggest land owners in this place. The Rajas perished but they persist.'

'Can you give some insights into the family?'

Shuabham watched his friend edge step by step.

'Well. Bhabendra Nath Thakur and his forefathers were men gifted with great honor and respect because of their knowledge. The family is blessed with wealth and wisdom. Rare combination and unique to this place.'

Poking a finger into his mouth in the most unkempt manner, Jogon began scratching his teeth to scrap off the residues of the rolls.

'Will it be possible for you to inform us about the close associates of Bodo Thakur? People like physician, lawyers et cetra, who could give us more information?'

'But, you met Nilikanta Thakur. Right?'

'Yes. But he didn't offer much, so we decided to come to you. Working at the Block Office, you must be in contact with large variety of people.'

'Yes. But you see Yash Babu, they are men beyond my reach. Altogether a different class. Further, the Thakur Bari is very particular in keeping their things within themselves. We usually don't tangle ourselves with their affairs. We are simple people. Most of the inhabitants of this part have their forefathers as boatmen or labourers. Lower class!' He smiled mockingly, 'You are gentlemen from city. Educated. But life out here is very primitive. Equality and upliftment is inked bold on papers, vague on land.'

'Got your point. How about a photo! My readers would like to see the source of this great piece of information.'

Jogon Rai's round brown face lit up. Straightening his shirt, rolling down the sleeves, adjusting the collar, he smiled wide displaying all his stained, unevenly arranged teeth for Shubham to click.

'I'll send you a copy.'

*   *   *

'Jogon deliberately elapsed. Maybe to avoid your uncle.'

Shuabham detested the use of the word 'uncle'.

'If only *Thakuma* knew the name!'

Shubham stared at his friend. Yash was scratching his stubbly cheeks vigorously as though the solution to the problem remained entwined in the black mess of his beard that he was trying to clip out with his fingers. He looked obsessed. Going to that extent to dig out the name of Bodo Thakur's legal advisor, could not be referred to as normal. But then Yash had been very fervent whenever he had the prospect to exploit his journalistic skills. It was his this quality that had brought them together.

'*Thakuma* may have got it wrong.' Shubham tried to divert him.

'You are sure, you did not receive or even been mentioned anything of the like, by your parents?'

'Positive!'

Flustered, Shubham looked outside the window regretting the lack of FM transmission in the village. At least, his friend's wild enthusiasm could have been curtailed for sometime by the melodious strings from the olden times.

The wheels of the car rotated in a manner similar to those of the taxi (black and yellow), that drove him to the hospital that day, some two and a half years back.

It had been a Monday; hot and torturous, with the Sun glaring down devilishly from the sky, he recalled. He had raced up the wide, tiled stairs to reach the second floor, E-Ward, Room No.204. The room was packed with people, mostly unfamiliar faces.

With all eyes pinned on him, he stumbled inside to stand next to the bed laced with equipments, where the body had laid, immobile; cold and quiet. He had clenched the edge of the bed; his white knuckles exhibited the tumult inside. On the bed lay stretched an open-mouthed, closed wrinkled-eyed, lifeless form of the man with whom his relation had been far from normal. Yet, he had felt empty; abandoned.

'Waited for you...but couldn't hold long'

A soft, sympathetic male voice had whispered into his ears.

The car took a sudden sharp turn, knocking Shubham on to the window panel.

'Aren't we going to the guest house?'

'To 'Raj Ghor'. My story requires little more detailing. Further, I am yet to relish the royalty of your blue-blood!' Yash winked.

'Blood has just one colour. It is always red!'

And it stinks.

The blood that had seeped out of his mother's blue veins was red; rather rancid black. He could not eat for days as the overpowering stink had saturated the air inside the house. And, there had been no escape.

The car danced to the beats from the radio on the macadamized road and the driver hummed with his idol saving Shubham some free, lonesome space to relax on their way back to Kolkata.

*   *   *

It was way past three, when the door bell twitted.

The lunch was over and the kids had retired to their respective undertakings. The distinguished manner in which the bell chirped told Mrs. Chatterjee that it had to be Shubham. She ran out of the kitchen as Kalki led him in and caught his eyes. They remained held to each other.

Dropping his bag on the floor, he walked over to her, still stuck to her gaze. The Goddess from his dream stood real, gorgeous in her mixed print silk sari; inviting and he moved towards her, like one under a spell.

'Good that you are back. I was worried.'

Her voice mellowed in him, making him realize how much he had missed her.

'How are you?'

'I am fine. You look tired!'

'I am sure...I'll be fine too with a cup of tea with you.'

She smiled. Her delicately arched lips enhanced the fineness of her face.

'Been to Thakur Bari?'

She asked igniting the stove and placing some water to boil.

'Yes. Met my uncle, Nilikanta Thakur.'

The name made her to turn around. How could she forget that name. The one, who had insulted her father publicly; who had caused them to weep for days; had shown no sympathy at her sister's demise. Rather typified it as an example for the rest to be careful before messing with them. Shubham called him "uncle". It pricked her.

Her thickly laced Piscean eyes bored into him. He noticed that her pupils were not typically black but a deeper shade of brown, complementing her fair skin.

'I am sorry!'

'For what?'

She asked confused.

'Nothing.'

He shook his head, denying. He couldn't bring himself to speak about her sister; to ask for forgiveness on behalf of his parents.

She didn't like the way he had reduced the significance of her inquiry. She turned to pour the steaming hot, teak coloured beverage into two ceramic mugs. Then, she placed them on the small table top that was fitted between the refrigerator and the door. After, she opened the overhead cabinet and took out a tin and laid some cookies on a plate next to the mugs. Next, she pulled two high stools from under the table and sat on one, leaving the other for him.

A smile drew to linger on his lips as his eyes followed her meticulous moves, in silence. Stepping in, he took the empty seat.

The descending, bright orange Sun streamed in through the ventilators kissing her face; her minute drop-shaped studded ear-ring sparkled against her jaw-line defining its contour. He noticed a tiny black mole just beneath her lower lip on the chin, by the edge of the lower jaw. The brownish tint of her hair was radiant under the rays, glistening her with an aura that of an angel; delicate, flimsy, surreal.

Yet, her long delicately curved nose, her prominent forehead, her bright velvety eyes, her smooth, fine skin, he could see everything clearly. She was real; as true as the Sun on the horizon; as the clouds in the sky; as the flowers on

the bush; as his heart, that began to beat in such an erratic
style; so loud, that he feared she could hear it.

'How old were you when you got married?'

She lifted her curtain of lashes to stare at him.

'Fifteen. Why?'

'You must have been very pretty then!'

A small smile pulled her lips apart to reveal a line of
beautifully arranged pearly teeth. He also saw a faint shade
of pink spreading over the pale yellow of her cheek.

Cradling the mug within the cup of her palms, she realized
that it wasn't just the tea that was hot; her face, her ears were
burning. She looked away to hide her awkwardness.

Hot fumes evaporating from her mug settled on her
skin, wetting it. Recollecting, she wiped it dry.

A quarter of a century ago, she had lived a similar dampness,
when she sat soaked in tears, by the news that she was to be
married to the same man who had been her sister's choice.
A bargain her poor, castigated father had accepted in terror
of social disgrace; afraid that none of his daughters might
get married ever, due to the prospective condemnation as
the groom's side had been adamant against taking his elder
one into their family anymore. They didn't want a radical
girl for a daughter-in-law.

Punished for being a girl's father, he was left with no
option but with whatever the groom's party was offering;
irrespective of how irrational it felt to him.

Mahua replaced Kakoli.

Clad in her sister's bridal wear, every inch of her body had
cried out protesting the rituals that marked the end of her

free days; that labeled her as owned and that too, by the man from her sister's dreams. She was a bride, bejeweled by the woes of destiny; her beauty overshadowed by the sorrows of misfortune that befell upon her family.

Nor had her sad mother appreciated her glowing skin, neither had her hungry mother-in-law valued her striking features. She had been busy encashing the stigma to the ultimate. On one hand, she had wringed out almost every possible rupee from her father as a compensation for showing mercy on such a ridiculed family, while on the other, she tactfully elevated her position amongst her people, portraying a selfless picture of generosity.

'After all, to accept a girl from such an ill-famed house, you need a big heart,' she had often laughed conceitedly to her guests.

Mrs. Chatterjee remembered to have been gifted with pity, disgust, scowls than praises.

His eyes were lazily roving on her face as his tone was fluid and his body, convivial. She couldn't stop being uneasy. No man had ever showered her approbation with such honesty and earnestly.

'Shubham, there is something I needed to discuss with you.' She brought herself to meet his gaze remembering her husband.

*   *   *

'Hey Shubham! When did you return?' Avni ran in to hug him.

'Just few hours.' Holding her lightly, he exclaimed, 'Congratulation!'

'Thank you!' She squeezed.

It was dark outside when the trio; Avni, Joy followed by their father had pushed inside.

'Shubham Da.'

Joy nodded his greeting. His hands were full with shopping bags. Shubham moved forward to help him.

'Good Evening, Mr. Chatterjee.'

'Good Evening.'

Shubham read the known indifference in his tone as he brisk passed him to hop upstairs. He retreated to the security of a beaming Avni and a weary Joy, complaining about his sister's freaky shopping mania.

'I can see you are all set!' He teased her.

'Yeah, of course! It's my wedding not birthday.' She returned equally.

'Now tell me. Is this 'would-be' of yours so compelling that you couldn't wait till the end of the term?' He winked.

'He is so rich!' She cried throwing her hands in air, 'And cute!'

Mrs. Chatterjee emerged from the kitchen just then. Her daughter's words made her to throw a look at her as she mounted the stairs.

'I don't like her when she does that!' Avni frowned pointing a finger at her mother. 'She doesn't approve of me leaving my course unfinished.'

'But she has a point.'

'Oh! Come on Shubham! How much will I earn? I'll end up being just a secretary! I have opted for a man who can fulfill all my dreams. He has promised honeymoon in Europe!'

'Your dreams are your responsibility, Avni!'

Mrs. Chatterjee's stern tone made them to look up. 'No one is going to fulfill them for you the way you want.'

She had had that discussion many times with her daughter, yet failed to change her thinking. Though she had vowed silence after their last conflict, she could not take her daughter's shameless presentation of the same to Shubham.

Shubham watched her awestruck.

'Dreams are our personal responsibility and no one can accomplish them for us.'

Mrs. Chatterjee had just taken words from his father's mouth; those, from his death-bed.

'Ohho Ma! Not again! Baba thinks it is fine to marry Raktim....then what is your problem?'

'Your attitude is a problem.....not for me but for you.'

Realizing the direction of the discussion, Mrs. Chatterjee preferred to disappear into the kitchen. She didn't want another unproductive clash; at least not in front of Shubham with her husband around.

'Why is she so oppressive!'

Avni demonstrated her anguish by shrugging her shoulders and rolling her big eyes.

'May be because she wants you to be independent. Not a burden on someone!'

'Hello!' Avni rejoined. 'I'll be leaving my house..my people. Will be giving myself out to him.....I am not a burden! I am doing him a favour.....He needs to look after me and my wishes. Fair deal! Right?' She said in a tight voice. 'They want a beautiful bride, I want a comfortable life!'

'So it is all about money!' He snapped.

'Everything is about money...darling!' She said smiling with a slack blink of her prominent eyes. 'What else are you imagining? Love!'

She raised her brows questioningly. 'You love one who makes you happy and happiness comes with a price tag attached to it. He wishes to gift me a solitaire ring. How could I not fall in love with him!'

Love. He twisted his lips evaluating her statement. Of course, Avni could not completely be rejected for her definition of love. You love one who makes you happy. He had been very happy with his mother. But she had left him behind alone. His love fell weak to keep her. Since then, he had become suspicious about the vigor of love; kept himself out of its way.

Yes. There had been few short-lived sources of pleasure though and he watched his latest source walk in, loaded with eatables for snacking.

'Have you been in love ever?' Avni asked.

'No.'

He had been always very clear about that; even when he wasn't living alone. He had turned his back on love every time without feeling sorry.

What is love? A rainbow, momentary....transient like soap-bubble....Unreal.

Playing with a hot *pakora* (fried dumplings), his eyes followed her, obliviously.

She was not just married but a mother of two grown kids. Not free like the others, but bound and out of reach. Yet, her every move was stealing a second from his time; causing him to peer at her. He knew it couldn't be love but she sure provided him with, not only gratification but a sense of belongingness. Her very presence made him feel extraordinary; special, as if each of her action was in relation to him, addressed to him.

Love or no love, it did feel great!

Sitting with her cup of tea and a magazine, far from Shubham, she had a very odd feeling that he was observing her; following her. It bothered her and she was not clear why it should. Why in that group of people, her brain seemed to pick up only the signals transmitting from him. In order to prove to herself that, all that was her wasteful imagination, that he was busy with the rest enjoying his snacks, she lifted her pair of eyes to look towards him.

His pair were laid welcoming on her shores. She withdrew hers' and looked away.

Something about the way Shubham had looked at her, disturbed her; made her conscious. Her body too had been causing her dilemma. She forced her brain to decipher the meaning of the lines printed on the page of the magazine while resolving to get an appointment with her doctor soon.

I am definitely getting old.

*   *   *

Tepid, he pulled the curtains to let the light break in. All his bags were packed and set. He lingeringly looked around at the room that had harbored his days and his nights; his conscious and unconscious mind; his truths and his lies.

'I'll preserve if anything is left behind. You can always come to collect later.'

Her voice made him to jump backwards. She was standing at the door. His half heart doubled in mass. He didn't expect her to be up so early. He had announced his departure the previous night to avoid exaggerated yet empty 'good-byes', especially at the door.

The air around was quiet; only the rhythms of their breathings, audible.

The woman from his dream was standing like a shadow against the dull background of a murky morning; irresistible, in her lavender sari with supple eyes and clasped hands. He couldn't help but cup them in between his palms.

'Thank you!'

All he could say for everything she had done for him.

She managed a smile. Heat from his flesh seeped into her veins and she drew her hands out from his grip, growing uncomfortable. Their proximity alarmed her and she stepped aside to create space.

He walked past.

Gopida followed with the luggage.

Mrs. Chatterjee stood fixed, astounded at the peculiar kind of impact the man had successfully inflicted upon her; both, at his entry and his exit.

She had been raw when he had landed that afternoon and wanted him to leave, as soon as he arrived. In a matter of two weeks, all that repulsion was spent, to grow a want, a strange longing; an ache, as she watched him fade away, out of the door.

Chapter 7

The cab picked up speed. The house began receding.

His mind flew back to catch a situation akin to the present one, some two years ago when he had left Mereline's residence one fine morning; his fair-faced, Caucasian boss from his first job.

He was a fresh, fine-arts photography graduate then who had joined as an under-trainee to a very reputed photographer, Mereline Price, in the heavenly hill-station of Dehradun. Sharing a British root, she was more Indian as she had lived there ever since her childhood.

Almost ten years more than him, she had been a woman laced with colossal knowledge and experience in the field of photography. An outright professional, she had been inflexible; difficult to elude or impress. She believed in labouring and made everyone in her studio slog. Like all, Shubham too had taken her to be a snob, initially. Smoking her long, thin, cocoa-coloured cigar, she would scrutinize every picture with an eagle-eye. Only a few would meet her standard, in a hoard. She had always vouched 'Freedom Of Expression' as the bottom-line for creativity.

Shubham had been trying hard like the rest, to meet her level.

One day, a car had skidded to stop in front of the studio and his father stepped out, spewing astonishment all across. He had then won his second National Award and had been all over print and electronic media as a modern, meaningful director, soon to be working at the international level. He had walked straight into her cabin after briefly interacting with him.

Soon after his father's exit, a shaken Shubham had been summoned by her to share her crushing excitement. Since then, she began treating him with little lofty interest; something, that he had loathed. It had caused him to become indifferent, disrespectful towards her.

'*What is the matter with you?*' She had demanded within the close doors of her chamber.

His broiling irritation against his father then, had made him to stay away, even from his shadow and he had expelled his agitation by blaming it on to her that she had been impressed by his identity as Niranjan Sarkar's son than acknowledging his efforts as a photographer.

'*What!*' *She laughed.* '*Oh my God!*' *She dragged hard on her cigar and puffed out a large circle of smoke in the air.*

'*Look at you. Crying like a boy. Pissing in your pants, are you?*' *She laughed again tapping the ash into the crystal bowl on her table.*

Pulling one more time, she crushed the stub, released the fume and crossed over to sit on the table next to his side.

'*I admit, I am impressed. People take advantage of any fame related to them. You are different. I like you.*'

Leaning forward on him, she said in her husky voice while stroking his hot cheek with her fingers.

'How about working with me! I need someone to help me with my project for the upcoming exhibition.'

Shubham's mouth fell open.

'And.....I and your father......just shook hands. Don't be so jealous...kid!'

She tapped on his flaming skin lightly, before releasing.

Their professional association soon developed a new dimension and became personal, so intimate that he had shifted in with her. His lack of faith in the institution of marriage in ally with the matured, practical approach of his partner had transformed the relation into an absolutely desirable one for him, in spite of the criticism and envy that surrounded it then.

Seven months into the relation, he had been pleasuring a smooth life, when one Saturday, he received a message.

'Father met with an accident. Is serious. Come urgently.'

His heart had sunk into his stomach. Shaking to his bones, he had made that call. Next, he had been on his way to Kolkata.

His father's death marked the beginning of the distance between him and Mereline and within three months, he had decided to call it off and move out of her apartment and her life.

*   *   *

The black and yellow taxi jerked to stop in front of an iron gate in a red-brick wall. On the right hand side of the gate was hung a copper plaque, on which were engraved some letters in black.

Niranjan Nibas.

House NO. 49

Dropping his luggage next to the gate, he ran the entire length of footpath that was lined with wild, untrimmed foliage creeping and crawling in every course suited. Few deodars, eucalyptus, spruce and tall fir lined the wall. He jumped up the stone steps and landed on the wooden porch, shaded by a planked roof-top.

The dark teak wood door unbolted. Ganesh rushed out to collect the luggage into the house.

Ganesh was one of Yash's trusted employee whom he had deployed in Niranjan Nibas to take care of Shubham and the house, during his stay. He followed Ganesh and entered a magnificent hall; red-bricked walls with giant curtain less windows letting the sunlight in uninterrupted, muddling the magnitude of its size. The furniture had been pushed to one corner and covered, to facilitate the work that had just finished under the supervision of Shyamal Das.

The hall bifurcated into two wings. The left wing housed the kitchen and the store. He crossed the hall and took the door to the right. It led him into a corridor which was lined up by rooms on each side. He walked past one room each on either side and unlocked the second door on the left. His bedroom, once yellow, now smelled of fresh paint in shades of blue. He walked over to open the windows to dilute the sturdy waft of petroleum floating in.

'Sahib, tea.'

A lady, Ganesh's wife came in followed by her husband carrying his belongings who dropped them by the wall next to the door.

'What would you have for lunch? Ganesh would get it from the market.'

Shubham nodded. They left.

Sipping hot tea, he sat examining the *Bangla* newspaper when his cell buzzed to life.

'Good Morning Mr. Sarkar. Shyamal here sir! Are you satisfied with the work?'

'Looks good!'

'You'll not regret. We will get a good bid.'

Shyamal Das went on to explain how much he and his team had taken pain to upgrade the ragged status of that considerably old construction. Shubham listened patiently while reading the advertisement the property dealer had put on the paper, for sale of the property. He sighed out loud. He was not clear if it was due to Shyamal's blabbering or his empty stomach that his head was splitting. Attributing it to the strong odor inside the room, he marched out holding the cup.

He entered the adjoining room. An equivalent room, once the guest room though, derisively he snorted out a laughter, no guest had ever used the room. Shyamal had painted it in purple. He inspected the work done for some time.

Next room, on the extreme right, opposite to the guest room, was a huge room, devoid of windows and was very dark. He switched the lights on, to see. A gigantic screen hung on one wall and few chairs were presently tucked in a stack, at a corner. It was a dull room which his father had used to screen his work for his friends and colleagues. Shubham had mostly stayed away from it.

Walking over to the portion of the wall that had the biggest patch of cement missing from it, he looked closely. It was covered up well. His father had smashed a wooden chair on to it, bringing down a considerable piece of it to dust, after that fatal argument; the last one that the house had witnessed.

It was his father's study, next. Avoiding it, he moved a few steps forward to reach the subsequent one on the line. He pushed in.

It was the brightest room in the entire house with four full windows looking out at the garden. He could smell wild flowers and eucalyptus. It was the music room; the room that nestled most of his memorable moments with his mother. They had sang together there.

Her face would glow, whenever she sang, he recalled. He had loved to imitate her and she would correct him where ever and whenever he went wrong.

The furniture here too lay huddled in a mess. His eyes caught a steel rod from amongst the clutter. Anxious, he pulled it out. It was one of the high steel chairs with leather seat that his father had brought for him. And Monalisa.

'This is for you.'

A beautifully wrapped elongated case was presented to him by his father on his sixteenth birthday.

'What is that?'

A very young Shubham asked, reluctant to touch that red and yellow packet.

'A violin.'

'A violin!'

Bewildered, he fought to keep his voice low. He didn't want a musical instrument when the person with whom he used to enjoy music, was no more.

'Your mother desired to gift you a violin this birthday.'

It was ludicrous. It had been just few months that his mother had deserted him because of that man, who now

stood holding a piece of lifeless wood pinned with few strings,
proclaiming posthumous promises.

'I don't want it!'

'Why?'

A pair of dark eyes stared at him, forebodingly.

'I don't know to play.'

He observed him awe-eyed, suppressing his pain.

How could he make a heartless man understand his ache.
After all, he did not lose much, rather gained name, fame and
recognition.

People no longer saw him as guilty. Their eyes were dazzled
by the sparkling star dust on him. But he wasn't blind and
won't spare him so easily. He would keep the fire burning;
would seek justice for his mother and himself, in his own way.

'Well then, I'll get you a teacher.'

*   *   *

A hand landed on his back. Startled, he swirled sharply
causing the cup in his hand to fly out and land crushing
on to the dark cemented floor, shattering into numerous
fragments that skidded in every direction.

'Oh! Sahib. It's just me!' Ganesh screamed. 'Your phone
sahib. It was ringing.' He held out the black handset.

Taking a grip on his racing heart, he took the cell from
Ganesh's hand; his thoughts battling with the ceramic
pieces that lay scattered by his feet.

Though the crash had not been aş loud and the bits,
not as big, it reminded him of his violin that he had flung
across the room at his father, with all his force. It missed

the target and had dropped smashing on the floor of his bedroom.

Teased by his raised temper, he marched out to settle in front of the study and banged the door open.

The poised room stared back; as though holding its breath, waiting impassive and unscathed.

The walls remained as hidden behind the rows of bookcases, cupboards and cabinets, as ever. Albeit, the calendars and posters were missing; probably scrapped off for painting. The huge wooden desk that his father had used, was set in the centre covered with a sheet like the rest of the furniture in the house. But, something was odd; missing. The big, brown sofa. The couch that his father had preferred to recline on, when thinking hard; the one, where she had sat talking to him. The one, where her shimmering body had laid intertwined with that of his fathers', in such an intimate position, as ever witnessed by his stark pair of young, bleak eyes.

His cell buzzed in his fist.
    'Dada!'

Withdrawing himself, both from the place and the captivating glimpses from his early life, he walked into the sanctuary of his room. Yash had called to check if he was fine. It was a very casual call but one that Shubham appreciated from the bottom of his heart. It regurgitated the precious treasure he possessed as a friend.

To soar his mood further, he received another call from his property dealer informing about the positive response the sale advertisement had generated.

'Hundred percent sure Mr. Sarkar! We are going to draw good money.'

*   *   *

'You are so lucky! You always have been!'

A thin, shrill voice squeaked out of a rather voluminous body, whose flaps of bloated belly were bulging out from the ties of her sari. Her round, pale face was anointed with prominent vermilion on her forehead and a dark red lipstick defined the contours of her lips which she had twisted in exasperation.

'You grabbed Pranab and now, your daughter could manage such a wealthy family. I am so worried about my Reema.' She sat occupying half of the king-sized bed examining the exhibits that lay scattered on the bed; jewelries, dresses, gifts, garments. 'Your planets seems to be nicely placed every time! How I wish my Reema gets a rich man too!'

'Raktim is a very good boy.'

Irritated by her ever complaining sister-in-law, Mrs. Chatterjee said affirming.

'Yes. I know. Pranab is so smart. Very clever! Not like Reema's father. Clumsy old man!'

'Don't worry Didi! Reema will get a good husband.'

Mrs. Chatterjee squeezed her sister-in-law's fat hand, sympathetically.

'How about Shubham?'

Avni jumped shaking her mother by shoulders.

'What about Shubham!'

Mrs. Chatterjee fought to restore her balance.

'Who is Shubahm?'

The fat lady yelped excitingly.

A thin, fair, lass dressed in a black frock, filing her toe nails, took her lazy eyes off from the filer and looked in the direction of the rest of the females in the room.

'Shubham Sarkar, *Pishi!* He is so cute!' Avni squashed her eyes and nose highlighting her words. 'He is just perfect for Reema.'

'Sarkar!' The enormous body shook vigorously, rocking the bed. 'How dare you ask me to give off my daughter to a man beneath me!'

'Ohho, *Pishi!* Be modern. We are already half a decade into the new millennium. People have literally soared to the sky. It's a digital world! You are still stuck to the stinking shit!'

Avni's reaction earned her mother a belligerent look from her aunt.

'Shut up! People might have soared to the sky but no one can survive without the basics. I can understand from where all this idiocy has poured into you!'

Mrs. Chatterjee refrained from counteracting. Her intelligence told her to let it pass like all those she had let go. To expect otherwise was foolishness. Rather, she got herself busy collecting the stuff from the bed and arranging them inside the wardrobe.

'Arrey! He is Niranjan Sarkar's son!'

Mrs. Chatterjee was amazed at her daughters' imprudence. She alluded a warning look at her. But Avni overlooked.

'He lives just few blocks from here.'

'And what does he do for living?'

The shrillness of the voice seemed to level down a bit.

'He is a photographer.'

'What!' Her jumbo body vibrated again. 'Mahua! Is this some kind of joke! You want my princess to live with a pauper!'

'No one is asking you to give your princess away to anyone!'

The deliberate stressing of the word 'princess' invited Mrs. Chatterjee a severe look from both, the mother and the daughter.

'Shubham is a nice guy.' She returned with pride.

She found herself countering in spite of the doggedness she had maintained all those years to stay away from useless confrontations.

'And a very good-looking one too.' Added Avni.

That was the last straw. The whole heap came tumbling down.

A pair of deep-set, bright eyes; a sharp nose; elongated cheeks pertaining to a strong jaw-line that furrowed into dimples when he smiled impishly; dark curls falling on the forehead, and those long, neatly rounded fingers that had clasped her hands; everything fell one after another.

Perplexed, she pushed the door of the wardrobe with a thud cutting his ghost out. She couldn't believe. He almost floated like a spirit.

A surge of adrenaline rushed through her veins and she hurried out of the crowd to escape in the quiet of her mind. What happened, had been occurring ever since he had left. She could feel him everywhere, in the hall, in the kitchen, on the terrace, in the lawn. Her afternoons were barren. Tired, she sat on a couch.

If only I could get everything back to normal!

Chapter 8

Dear Shubh,

This is very strange. I have never written to you before. But I am left with no choice. I may not get you in time to talk. Further, I have this faith that you won't discard this as you normally snub my words. We have long lost the track to good conversation and it is sad that we have never really put in enough effort to mend it.

Son, I am aware of your dissatisfaction and regrets against me and I accept, that partly, I am responsible. I couldn't spare enough time for you. But Shubh, I want you to understand that you were young and troubled. You wanted to leave and I had let you go, not because I wanted to get rid of you. But because I thought that a little fresh air would do you good. And when you were a little more grown, a little more man, we would have sat together to sort our differences out. I was only buying time for both of us. And here, I committed my gravest mistake. I laid my trust on time yet again knowing that time is no one's friend. It neither waits nor cares. It had failed me with your mother. It failed me again. And I am left with none, to bargain.

Shubh, I am just an ordinary man, with limited attributes. Like others, I too wanted to prove my existence to the world. But tonight, as I lay counting my beats on a machine in this grave hospital room, assured that the life I had been so engrossed in is ticking away, I feel lonesome. How I wish you were here. I am missing you very much.

I don't have anything to present to you tonight except one piece of advice. Shubh, it is very important to have dreams. They give direction to our lives. Dreams are our personal responsibility and no one can accomplish them for us the way we can. It makes us feel worthy.

But one thing is even more important. Understanding our own self while chasing the stars. We should always keep in mind who we are, for this determines the path we choose. The man we become.

Life is bountiful. It provides you with enormous choices. But you should choose one that satisfies you from within. Only then, can you live the life fearlessly, with passion. I have always believed in it. Try it out. You won't regret.

Take care son!

The same old nothingness slid in, heaving his heart. He stowed the letter back on the stack and slammed the folder close.

Hadn't it been for Yash, he wouldn't have let the serpent out. It was his consistent nagging that Shubham had sat inspecting the legal documents relating his inheritance to check if the Will lay undetected somewhere in the pile of papers. The bundle included papers related to the house on sale which his father had purchased in 1981 from some Dev Dutta; documents regarding his office in Tollyganj; and few others but he found no Will. In its place, the note popped out; the one that had poisoned his mind and had sucked every drop of easiness out of his life.

'How could you be so forgetful?'
Mereline's cry resounded inside his head.
She had slammed a sealed packet on the desk that he was supposed to have dispatched.
'Your recklessness caused me to miss out on my entry into the exhibition!' She screamed pacing to and fro in the cabin. 'For God's sake, say something!'
He pressed his temples shutting his eyes. The veins supplying them inflated as though about to split open.
'Shubham, I am tired! Please take hold of your life. We can't go on like this!' She sank close to him on the couch.

He yanked his eyes open and turned to his right in a start, almost expecting Mereline next to him.
In contrast, his blank face stared back at him from the mirror on the door of his cupboard. There, at the back, he saw the naked window eyeing him, from behind as well.

The curtains had been removed to avoid spoilage during painting. He pulled out a bed sheet from inside the cupboard and covered it. He had an uncanny feeling of a pair of eyes boring into through them.

Replacing the folder back on the desk, he straightened himself on the bed. He retained the white light falling from the elongated tube on, for clarity of vision and mind. His father had statured dreams to decide the course of life. But the ones that followed his father's death had derailed him; had tortured him nights after nights resulting in a splitting head and nasty temper the following day.

The compartment was compressing; the smell taking over his brain. His senses were wearing out. But he wasn't struggling. Holding on to his depleting breaths, he waited for the sealed chamber to undo into endless meadow; for the red to dilute into florescence; for the nauseating odor to change to rose; the one she wore in her bun on her nape. And it happened.

Purple sky, blue grass; the Sun descending by the sphere. She stood with her back on him; rays washing her hair. He encircled her with his arms around her from behind. Everything was perfect; just the way he wanted. Relaxing, he dropped his chin to rest on her shoulder.

My dream!

Far, at the end; at the line joining the land to the heavens, he saw a shadow rising. Slowly, it began taking a form. A shape. A human shape! A known one. It began expanding; engulfing everything around; including them. Tall, distorted; yet defined.

Mr. Chatterjee? No! Baba?

He was rooted. Unable to move. His hands free of her now. She was leaving; walking away. He called out; cried. But she kept thinning, until she vanished in the dark.

*   *   *

The house was swarming with faces; all unfamiliar. He cruised through to see if he could discover a known island to port.

'Avni!'

He spotted her in a group of youngsters and waved his hand to get her attention.

'Hey Shubham!'

She leaped out of the crowd and landed next to him in no second.

'Looking great!'

He pulled his thumb up indicating towards her ravishing Prussian blue gown with black metal studded neckline.

'Raktim's choice!'

He rejoined her with a big smile while scanning for his lookout.

'Come.'

She caught hold of his hand and pulled him.

Dragging him along, she took him to the sitting place created by the side of the main staircase by spreading mattresses on the floor. It was teeming with women of every age, colour, and size.

'*Pishi!*'

A full sized robust lady responded in a thin voice that made him wonder if she was choking.

'Shubham.'

Avni pushed him to land on the mattress next to her.

'Ok. This is the guy. Not bad!'

Confused, he turned to look up only to find Avni missing.

'I am so troubled. This is my daughter.'

The huge lady pulled a hand out from the lot, hauling a girl who appeared to be made of paper. Light and handy.

'I wish to get a good, handsome, wealthy Brahmin boy for her. It is such a pity, I cannot accept you.'

Drawing his brows in a line, he studied both, the mother and the daughter trying to grasp the state of affair. Surprising, as it was to him to find that he had just been struck out of the matrimonial column by a complete stranger,as it was hilarious. It was insane. He hardly knew them.

'Can you get me one good groom for her!' Her marble eyes bored into him, 'You must be knowing few!'

'I am really sorry...I don't!'

'Don't lie!' She screeched. 'Some friend? Neighbour?'

'Aunty...I am getting late.'

He jumped to his feet.

He had sighted her, gawking at him from the other end of the hall.

No sooner had he balanced himself on his feet, a strong hand fisted around his arm and pulled him down.

'Look at her! Isn't she beautiful! And she sings melodiously.'

Maintaining her firm hold on his hand, she ordered her daughter to sing.

The thinner version of the bulky mother, started instantaneously, shrieking nodes in every possible range in her knowledge, matching her frail body to quaver like a dry leaf fighting to hold on, against the wind.

Shocked, he observed the duo in horror, thinking hard to device a way out. And the only way was to guarantee his support.

The aunty wasn't an easy prey. She made him revise her requirements three times; took his contact number and promises, that he would pick her calls; that he should be ready with few options when she would contact him in next ten days; that the details must have photographs and contact numbers of the prospective grooms. Pledging that he would take it up seriously, he could finally free himself to concentrate on what he had come for.

She was gleaming amongst a cluster of dull counterparts. He waited patiently, savoring his eyes on her spectacle.

'You are very busy! I can see!'
He taunted as she emerged from the crowd.
'You were busy too. I saw!'
Her mystified look hooked him. He smiled. All his uneasiness was thankfully a waste.
'They are your guests. I couldn't possibly be rude.' He winked playfully.
'Thank you!'
Mrs. Chatterjee walked passed.
He followed pleasingly.

He wasn't a man to believe in dreams or take them for inklings from the sixth sense. They were nothing more than mental manifestations of subconscious mind. Yet, the attendance of Mr. Chatterjee and his father in his dream alarmed him; though, he wasn't clear if one or both had been there.

He came to check if his fortress still stood steadfast or had fallen and changed alliance in his absence.

He was happy; it was safe. But, was unlike her usual self.

'What's wrong?'

'Nothing.'

Mrs. Chatterjee speeded. There were a ten and thousand things, not correct. One for instance was Shubham himself. As if haunting her in ethereal form wasn't enough, he had popped out of blue, in flesh and bones to intensify her condition.

And, found her beloved sister-in-law to befriend!

'Then, why are you so cross?' He paced to block her way.

She lowered her gaze, scared, he might perceive what resided hidden.

'Bye Shubham!'

Avni waved at him from the door.

'Where is she going?'

Shubham asked.

Condoning her disapproval, her biggest reason of worry was going out to get a diamond ring from Raktim, who was yet not knotted to her officially. And that too, on the day when she was asked not to leave the house by their family astrologer, whom her father was devoted to.

'Hey! Are you with me?'

She was startled by his fingers snapping on her face.

Without responding, she crossed him again.

'Fine.' He called out. 'Then...I should be leaving when you are so unavailable.'

*   *   *

She had not turned to his words; just walked away. His dream felt real.

The Tulika Ice-cream parlor, near Yash's office, was a cozy, happening cafe that remained busy from morning till midnight. However, it was most crowded during the afternoons. Young couples spawned secret amorous operations behind the tables in its dark interiors, safe from the outside callous world, by thick, flinted glass barriers.

A young boy was enjoying his girlfriend with a chilled mug of ice-cream, opposite to him.

'Kids aren't kids anymore.' Yash commented. 'Teens! Most vulnerable! The impact lasts long.'

Tracing the rim of his coffee mug with his finger, Shubham gulped the comment down endorsing it within. Who could had been more a victim of the truth. His mother, his father and Monalisa, all had happened to choose his teens to persecute him; afflict him such that the impact though not as overpowering but pertains, till date.

And she, had augmented it by behaving in compliance to his fears. Had his father conspired yet again to hurt him by snatching away his joy. He had done it before; not once or twice but thrice. Both in his life and with his death, he had taken away all those he was close to; Ma and Monalisa, in his life and Mereline, when dead. And had left him drifting, until he found her docks. Had his father's spirit visited his dream to mock at his inability to stand up against him, he wondered.

'Sir, would you like to take something for your loved ones. We are providing a complimentary service to all our valued customers.'

A flat- faced girl in red and black uniform parroted out her line in a monotonous tone pasted with an artificial smile.

'You can get a love message written on any of our confectionary, along with a red rose.'

Yash made the payment crying, how he regretted the absence of a woman in his life and went out to get his first love out of the parking.

'Can you cream a smiling face on that black forest?' Shubham requested pointing into the glass display.

'Sure.'

'What's that ?' Yash questioned as soon as he entered the car.

'Evening snack!'

He lied hoping that his friend won't notice that big, red rose on the top of the paper box through the transparent polythene bag.

Yash's side glance corrected his doubt. He was quick; had always been.

'Relations do not end this way. You have to understand. She has to run that place.' Yash urged.

'She can run her place. She isn't my boss anymore. She lives with me. I deserve to be respected.'

'You live with her!' Yash reprimanded tightly. 'And she is your boss, take it or leave it.'

'Fine. Then she can be the boss. I resign to be her subordinate!' An angry, puffed-eyed Shubham yelled.

Yash and Mereline had been old acquaintances. It was during the budding days of their relationship when Mereline Price had been acknowledged for her work in collaboration with an upcoming painter, in an exhibition organized to promote the blooming feminism in the country, under the banner 'MODERN WOMEN OF INDIA' and Yash had come to cover the event, that she got Shubham introduced to Yash as a co-worker. However, she hadn't forgotten to lay open his identity. The name Niranjan Sarkar infected Yash and ever since, he stayed in touch.

Though Shubham wasn't aware if they were still in contact, for Yash had never mentioned her and he never bothered to ask.

*   *   *

The wroth iron gate rested wide open. He walked in. A large number of people, like a school of fishes, swam in bundles in various directions about the house, inside out. Some were busy rearranging the lawn to cater space; some, planting stilts for erecting tent; some other, lining the exterior of the house with lamps and colourful bulbs.

A bunch of women were gathered in front of the house, busy chatting. He swept passed them and was about to push the ajar door wide when he heard the harsh words of Mr. Chatterjee bombarding someone with instructions. After his ambiguous encounter with the man in his dream, he didn't want any more bitterness. But delivering the parcel was important.

'Excuse me!'

He made one of the known lady to turn.

He had often seen her at the house chitchatting with her like good friends. Persuading her to hand the parcel only to its prospective owner was a little effortful as she was very reluctant to leave her committee.

While dragging his feet backwards step by step, he waited lingeringly, hoping to see her. He wanted to be sure, his dream wasn't a vision.

But, she didn't appear.

'Mahua...This is for you!'

'What is this?'

A white and pink paper packet with a glossy, fragrant rose, came out of the polythene to puzzle her. As she opened the box, a fat slice of dark chocolate pastry smiled creamy white at her.

'Wow!'

Arundhati blew her lungs out.

'Who gave you this?'

'That boy who lived with you? Met me at the door. Was very particular that it should reach only you!'

Arundhati's prying statements highlighted her suspicious mind, working in the making of a fabulous gossip.

'I asked him. For Avni.'

She smiled bright to erase her friend's qualm. Arundhati showed her teeth too.

'Oh! What a lovely flower!'

A plump hand tore the rose ruthlessly from the box where it was sellotaped and poked it in her bun.

'What's in it?...Cake!'

Without waiting for any answer, she cut into the heart of the cake and axed out a considerable amount to stuff her mouth with.

'They use brandy to make these things swell to this softness!'

Mrs. Chatterjee couldn't read if her sister-in-law was complaining, gossiping or was zealous about the idea of use of alcohol in the pastry, but she definitely cherished it inside her mouth.

A nerve at the back of her neck began pulsating vigorously. She pressed it to hold the rising anger inside. It was her gift and she couldn't even get to see it properly; was just watching it being mutilated heartlessly.

'When is Avni coming back? I told you not to let her out today!'

The vigor of the voice was much more threatening than her excited nerve. She had fabricated the truth; had enveloped her daughter's extravagant date with an unavoidable appointment with the dentist, to make it more logical and acceptable to her husband. And hoped that Avni would play along; visit the doctor and get the scaling done if she wanted her planets to be in right quarters, at least with that of her father's.

'Mahua.' Her sister-in-law followed next, 'You could not administer discipline in your daughter. She should have at least respected Guruji's words! What if...this whole thing snaps and falls apart?'

'Didi....Isn't Avni anything to you?' She condemned fiercely.

Her sister-in-law pecked the crumbs from the box, dropped it inside the polythene that still hung in Mrs. Chatterjee's hand and walked away, indifferently. It pricked her but her perkiness was more due to her daughter.

The Bhattacharjees might not approve of her fervent, careless attitude. Knowing them, an over smart, ultra modern bride might not go well down their throats.

Chapter 9

An elaborate marquee was erected taking in the entire length of the lawn from the front gate extending up to the back via the side of the house. An ethnically decorated *'Chandnatolla'* (wedding alter and canopy) was built inside. The marriage commenced with the auspicious *'Ashirbaad'* (blessing ceremony).

The otherwise poised, sophisticated Mrs. Battacharjee was thrown off balance by the glitter of the sparkling diamond of a commendable size on Avni's finger. The tightness of her facial muscles, when she asked Avni to remove it so that she can be adorned with the ornaments from their side, made Mrs. Chatterjee wonder if she knew, where that gem had come from. However, Mrs. Chatterjee didn't let the encouraging smile wade off from her face, when her daughter pulled it out grudgingly and handed it over to her.

It was just the beginning for her daughter; life's real tests still awaited.

The ceremonial rites and rituals followed one after another. During the occasion of *'Gaye Holud'*, when the bride is smeared with fresh turmeric paste to improve the radiance of her skin, Mrs. Chatterjee gaped at her girl with moist eyes remembering the day when she was born.

Young at seventeen, how she had been transformed into a mother from a woman, in one moment; how she had spent sleepless nights, so that her baby could dream; how she forgot to cry at her woes but tried to read happy stories in her baby's doodling.

And there she was, a grown adult, gleaming in yellow turmeric, smiling, enjoying, feeling important.

*   *   *

Her lack of acknowledgement hurt him and Shubham decided to stay away for the initial days. It would give him time to get over the pang. Further, the preliminary rituals were very personal-type and he didn't want to throw himself amongst the relatives, especially those of Mr. Chatterjee's. And he knew that she would be completely unavailable. He didn't want another frustrating encounter to leave him dry and coarse.

As an alternative, he devoted the time to a more practical issue that was yet to be sorted out; the belongings in the house. Every room of the house had infinite things that required to be packed and removed before letting the house to the new owner. The worst being the study. Dreading the monstrous work required to sort, store or discard the numerous files and documents, he opted to begin clearing the shelves and cabinets in the hall, off his father's seals of achievements.

Since his small apartment in Mysore was not blessed with such space as to grace the presence of those unrewarding items, he had arranged a room in Yash's outhouse to store them as for now. He could get them anytime, once he had bought his own studio and started off independently. And to accomplish that, he needed money and those things, needed to be out of the house.

He didn't nurture great affection for the trophies and awards he had been storing so delicately; he just could not plausibly leave them at the mercy of a stranger.

'Dada!'
Yash was at the other end.
'Do you know anyone named Akheel Dasgupta?'
'No!'
'Well. He is a lawyer. Wishes to meet you!'
'Why?'
'He gave me his address. He wants to talk to you in person. Was referring to our visit to Nilikanta.'

The name sent tremors to run beneath his skin.
Nilikanta's lawyer?

'Gave me tomorrow's appointment.'

Shubham calculated fast. He had punished himself much beyond tolerance. He had to see her. He must affirm himself of her acute acquiescence to him, before his departure, to conquer the coast.

And it was Avni's main marriage ceremony, the next day. Perfect juncture to get some private time with her. The public manner of the event would dilute the discrete nature of their association.

'Dada...can we start early? Say...by six in the morning?'
'Why?'
That roar clearly signed exasperation.

'It's Avni's wedding tomorrow.'

He tried to sound reasonable.

The line went mute. He could only hear the air ruffling through the wire.

'Avni's wedding!'

The words cracked open not just the lameness of his excuse but also ascertained him of his friend's annoyance at the finding.

'Of course.'

He pretended serious.

'Let's see.'

The line finally disconnected and he exhaled noisily back into the world of papers he was sorting in his father's study, feeling alive; similar to that hare, that managed a thin escape from under the claws of a hungry tiger.

*　　*　　*

Sharp at six, a car pulled in front of his house. Shubham jumped out of his bed. He had not expected Yash to be so prompt after his inflexibility the day before. Pushing into a pair of fresh trousers, he ran to occupy the passenger's seat.

'After all, it isn't a bad idea to start early. Relaxed traffic.... You see.' Yash ignited the engine. 'And I am invited too!' He vexed the car into life. 'Need a break from Priyanka.'

'Priyanka?'

Shubham turned stridently.

He wasn't aware of this aspect of his friend's life. Yash had never revealed his love life.

'Don't get ideas! She is my boss. And thinks.....I am rude....Not to notice her otherwise!'

The pinch of biting wit in his friend's tone made him laugh.

'Well, Avni's *pishi* needs a rich Brahmin boy for her daughter. You are Brahmin.'

'But not rich. Still stuck to my old-fashioned coupé!' Yash said stroking the steering wheel lovingly.

'That's because you want to. And you have a rich father.'

'Then get her hooked to my father. He is a wealthy Brahman who is very... experienced!' He winked, smiling mischievously.

The car wheeled on the same road they had traveled just a few days back. Within an hour and half, they reached the district town of Banipur. It was yet to gear in momentum. The market was empty. The shutters of the shops were down and locked. Only a few roadside tiny, portable stalls were selling hot tea with biscuits and cakes.

Acquiring a clear direction to the address, they drove passed an internationally approved educational institute; few colleges, schools; some government buildings.

Soon, they zapped onto a road under repair. Mountains of mud, rubble, stones lined the narrow lane that was left for use which took them to their destination.

The gate opened into a small but well manicured lawn with sufficient space for vehicles to turn and park. The parapets were very high and hid the house from outside world. Flowers were planted along the border of the inner side. The entrance of the house was guarded by iron grill.

Yash pressed the door bell on the wall beside the grill. A man emerged from inside the house. Round faced; grey haired; his well maintained body was clad in a pair of comfortable pajamas and a shirt.

'Mr. Akheel Dasgupta?'

Yash asked through the bars.

'Yash Bharadwaj?'

The man responded.

'Good Morning, sir.'

They were escorted into a well furnished living room that hung a big artistically done portrait of Sri Rabindranath Tagore in a gold frame.

'So you are Swarnali's son!'

The informal manner in which the man uttered his mother's name suggested Shubham, a very close association. And why shouldn't be, if he was Nilikanta's lawyer; the fact that intrigued his patience.

'You wished to talk to me in person.'

'Yes. I was curious to see the person who provoked the unfazed Nilikanta to make such an absurd move.'

Shubham had always resented the double-standard stance projected so casually by these people in black and white. They never stop playing the 'I know it all' game, terrifying the common mob, handicapping them, first, psychologically and then, monetarily. It couldn't just be his curiosity that made him to excavate them out.

'You look more like your father...I must say.'

He continued.

'You knew him too!'

Shubham was getting very anxious now. What business Nilikanta's lawyer had with his father when they didn't see each other, eye to eye.

'Met him once. He had come to me. Soon after Swarnali's demise. After that....he became a big man. Out of reach.'

'Why did he come to meet you?'

The specificity of the mentioned time of his father's visit triggered his brain cells. He clearly remembered what all had followed after. What he heard now was a news.

Mr. Dasgupta stood up and walked over to a tall cabinet and pulled out a drawer. Taking a file out of it, he returned back to his seat and pushed the file towards Shubham.

'To return this!'

'What's this?'

Shubham took up the brown coloured hard paper file and unfolded it. Inside was a hundred rupees stamp paper, documented into a legal authority. He began reading.

The Will!

Handing it over to Yash, he gaped at the lawyer trying to understand the game.

'You knew about it?'

The lawyer asked twisting his lips into a crooked smile.

'Yes. I did.'

He didn't want to fall a bait to a lawyer's trap. He knew, they fed on ignorance.

'And it was with Mr. Sarkar?'

Yash gushed out his disbelief.

'Very much. I had gone personally to deliver it to Swarnali on Bodo Thakur's death. It was his last wish.'

'Then why Mr. Sarkar returned it?'

'Well. I am not aware of the reason. But yes...when asked he said...he didn't want to leave any problem trailing behind.'

The lawyer nodded.

Shubham still remained entangled, trying to unknot the stranded strings, the man was curling up.

'One thing Shubham...If you have known about it...then why didn't you ever come to get it? Or are you like your father? Self-respecting and proud!'

Shubham didn't feel like answering that question.

'We came to know about it just a few days back.'

The sinisterly smile broadened.

'I don't doubt...it wasn't Nilikanta who told you about it?'

The sentence was an interrogatory one. The kind Shubham disliked most; trying to squeeze things out against one's will.

'That should not be your concern.'

The lawyer crouched with a squeezed forehead and studied Shubham for sometime before responding.

'But Shubham....it is soon going to be your matter of great concern!'

Shubham peered at Yash.

'Nilikanta has filed a petition claiming legal ownership of the entire Thakur property declaring himself the only living heir...Including that!'

Yash had a 'I told you' kind of look on his flustered face.

'And you made us drive all the way from Kolkata to inform about a law-suit!' Yash rejoined. 'You could have done that over phone.'

'I couldn't have given you that..over phone.'

He pointed towards the file on Yash's lap.

The man seemed to love mocking at every point, relevant or not.

'But Why? Being Nilikanta's lawyer... why are you giving this thing to us? Is it a copy?'

Yash began inspecting the file to ascertain its authenticity.

'No Mr. Bharadwaj. This is original. I had documented it. Under Bodo Thakur's instruction.' He paused seriously.

'And...I am not Nilikanta's lawyer. He has his own band of crooks. One of them led me to this piece of information that someone had shaken his nerves loose. I did a little digging and Jogon Rai popped out.'

Shubham found if difficult to believe that the man just wished to help him.

'In that case...thank you very much!'

Gathering the file in his possession, he stood upright.

'Shubham. I am not finished yet!'

That's it!

He knew. They were not easily finishing type of people. They always had a catch.

'I can take the case on your behalf. But I have a condition. I win....I get the property!'

'What?'

Yash jumped.

'Don't worry. I'll buy it from you. Your price. My words. No bargain.'

'And what if you lose?'

At this, the man gave out a short lived laughter opening his whole mouth unveiling till his epiglottis, scoffing at Yash's words.

'I lose....you pay me nothing.' He bit his lip for a second, examining them. 'But I can guarantee you victory. I know Nilikanta better than he knows himself.'

'And why? Why should I sell it to you? What is your interest?'

Shubham was sick of the mysteriousness of the matter.

'My interest!' He shot up and walked over to the grilled window on the opposite. 'Shubham, my forefathers had been serving this family for ages. My father was a lawyer too and was trusted with the legal matters of the Thakurs. I followed my father. Had worked for Bodo Thakur for more than a decade. Had seen your mother grow up.' He turned to face him. 'She was Bodo Thakur's heart and soul. Even after that unacceptable behaviour of hers...Bodo Thakur could not cut her out completely. And during his failing years...he asked me to document that...declaring a substantial plot of land to her and from her...to you as her inheritor. He kept it with me. Secret. Didn't trust Nilikanta. But he came to learn about it...Most probably from your mother. She was devastated and very furious with him for not informing her about her father's illness and subsequent demise.' He came back to stand next to Shubham.

'Nilikanta took out his frustration on me. Since then...I don't have any connection with him. But...it still hurts. You see...this piece of land at present harnesses his major harvest...Finances the supremacy and grandeur he exhibits and uses to harass people. My interest is in his downfall.'

Vengeance. Shubham felt a fine cord of it vibrating inside him as well, recollecting his own episode with his uncle.

'Shubham...this is your property. And you have the absolute right to deal with it the way you desire. But don't forget two things. One...that you'll have to get a lawyer as soon as possible if you want to retain the property. You don't have much time. Second...you are up against a man who is not only greedy but cunningly influential!'

Straightening up, Yash walked to join them.

'I'll take the case...free of cost but my clause stands firm.'

*   *   *

'Why did you go there when I asked you not to?'

His father demanded in a full, hoarse voice so loud that it seeped out through the sealed doors.

Shubham was standing outside in his dirty school uniform waiting to be attended by his mother. Instead, he heard her crying.

'You must give it back!'

His father's ear-bursting shouts were countered by weak sobs from his mother.

'No! This is a blessing for my son.'

At that moment, something came tumbling down on to the floor, inside the room.

'You have never listened to me! Have never cared for me! You were in a situation.....and you wanted to escape. You used me! You needed someone..... and it could have been anybody. I happened to be there! Like a fool! Fine.... From today onwards...I set you free. You live your way.... and I'll not ask. You can go anywhere you want...... or do anything you desire...... But...you too lose your hold on me and my life...... I'll live my life my way. It should be of no concern to you...what I do....where I go! Today.... I regret that you are a part of me!'

Kicking the door open, his father crossed him in furry, not noticing him standing in the way and entered the dark room. Next, he heard a high-decibel crash cracking out from the room.

That night, his father had not returned home. A tormented Shubham had waited into sleep, hoping to see his mother emerge from behind the closed doors of her bedroom. The following day, he had been awakened by the chaos in the house. Rubbing his eyes, he had gone into the adjacent room trying to figure the cause of that bedlam.

The room had been pouring with people; some in orderly uniform. His father had been there too, sitting, head down, on the floor at a corner, surrounded by some men. Fighting his way in, as he moved closer, his heart had begun drumming inside his chest. And then, his eyes had caught the glimpse.

A pool of thick, slimy blood, smelling rotten, had been collected down there, where a hand was hanging from above the bed, on which his mother's blanched body lay across. The light coloured bed sheet had been stained dark; crimson, rather black. He had frozen, hit by the view.

His father had come running to cover him but, he pushed him away and had ran out trembling in pain, agony, fear and wrath; sheared in abhorrence.

'See, meeting Jogon Rai didn't go waste! We got it!

Yash was singing merry song. The car was speeding towards Kolkata.

'Now we can enjoy the party to its ultimate!'

Shubham wasn't of the same opinion. He had lived a decade conjecturing logic for the series of events that preceded and succeeded his biggest loss. Though still wooly, the last nail of the coffin was in his hands. The dictum, the Will that announced him a rich man, was what his parents had been in conflict about, that evening before. How on earth, could he be happy about it. Further, if he didn't act fast, it might not remain his at all.

'Why are you so pissed off? Don't worry. We'll find some way out.'

His friend patted his back encouragingly. Shubham stared back smiling, wondering if he would feel the same if he had known all the facts related to the piece of paper that was the root to all his sufferings; would be as pleased if he had thrived all that, that sub-sequenced his mother's suicide.

The enquiries he had been subjected to, not only from the authorities but from everyone around; his teachers, school mates, neighbours, peons, watchmen, almost all seemed to be pitilessly interested to know if the rumors were correct. That his father had killed his mother because he was in an affair outside the marriage or the other way around, where his father murdered her due to her infidelity or she had committed suicide due to his father's disloyalty or she killed herself as she wasn't a chaste lady and was caught, et cetra, et cetra. His nights had been stretched long as he lay awake, staring at the ceiling, trying to digest the insensitivity people pushed down up on him, disregarding his distress.

Season had changed from spring to summer, so had his father's position. He had come out clean from the investigation and one of his films had beaten the scrutiny and criticism of the jury to mark its excellence. He had become a name. The media, which had been so far busy digging into the dirt of his personal life, started singing his brilliance in public. He was no more a villain but had become a hero; still a hot topic but on the positive scale.

Lonely, a fifteen year old Shubham had loathed to be stopped and showered with flowery words by those, who had not held their tongue while ripping him, just few days previously; and that too, regarding a man who may had been given a clean chit by the law, was still his prime culprit. The ultimate murderer; one who had killed not with a weapon, but with his words. A smart slaughter; no clue, no evidence to prove the crime.

'Shubham! Do you still need to sell your house now that you are loaded?'

'I am not selling it just for money!'

Yash's sermons had been a constant, ever since he had failed to streamline his professional life after Mereline. His whimsical, incoherent living had let a lot to slip between his fingers; a ground for his friend to harangue him now and then.

'Whatever! That's your house! Call the sale off.'

That's my father's house!

A gallery to exhibit his achievements. He was confined to only one room; his bedroom. However, he had exploited the music room quite often, when his mother had been there. And, for few more days with Monalisa.

It was two days after his sixteenth birthday, on 19 February, when a maid had ushered him into the study, a thin, tall, shabby Shubham had found his father drawn in a polite conversation with a lady, more precisely, a very young lady, whose shiny red top was glittering against the dull brown sofa she had sat on; her crossed lanky legs, appeared creamy and smooth, from under her black skirt. Her face, round like moon had two small, thin, chinky eyes, shining like black pearls against her white skin and her long, straight, silky hair was spread on her hip like water, luminous down a fall.

'Meet your teacher.' His father had said calling him in.

The girl shifted her look on him.

'Hello!'

She extended her delicate hand which he had hesitantly accepted. She had smiled. The boring room had lightened, cheering every entity inside, including his obstinacy. And his sixteen year old heart had sailed out, anchored to its magnetism.

She had been an excellent violin teacher; expert, maneuvering the instrument with ease and grace. In contrast to her deceptive tender looks, the fineness of her stick on the strings, proclaimed genuine ingenious, that of a maestro; enough for his feral, raw emotions to fall a prey to the ravishing Monalisa and her enticing enigma.

'You are good!'
She would often say in her silky voice, wreaking limitless pleasure and he would gear up every time to perform even better to impress her all over again.

To traumatize his teen temper even further, there had been an additional input of close physical contacts; touches that his pure, unscathed body had not lived so far.

A gentle push lifting his back; feathery strokes adjusting his face on the chin-rest; downy taps on his collarbone, chest shifting the violin in position; light squeezes on his arms to make him hold it correctly. Or, a complete embrace from behind, pressing her soft front on to his back, stiffening every strand of muscle in his body, as she worked with his fingers on the fingerboard instructing some difficult nodes.

A light pull of his ears; a gentle squeeze on his nose; her loving fingers circling his curls on his forehead in jest, would put his heart racing at an abnormally high pace.

'Perfect!'
She had screamed once besieged by his errorless tuning and moved over to plant a moist, fiery kiss just by his mouth with her pink, hot lips.

That night, he remembered, he had slept deep and sound, without the ghouls of loss and loneliness crawling from under the mosquito-net, on to the bed, along with him.

'Think about it. Your early life breathes in there.'
My early life stinks in there!
His first crush; his Juliette, had chosen to get herself manned by his father in there, on that sickening sofa.

*   *   *

The *'Bor Jatri'* (the groom's party) arrived and were welcomed by sprinkling trefoil and husked rice from a winnow. Mr. Chatterjee then offered his son-in-law new clothes to change into, a custom preceding the marriage. Arrival of the groom increased the commotion as everyone wanted to have a glimpse of him; of the man who was destined to be the owner of the bride's life, so that they can create their individual opinions for future gossips.

The ceremony commenced. Heavily made up Avni was lifted on the *Pidi* (wooden stool), by her brother and cousins and circled around Raktim seven times with her face hidden by betel leaves which she slowly and shying removed, to render him with a loving look.

Shubham stood with Yash in a black embroidered *kurta*, a golden *dhoti* and a light brown shawl, amidst the hooting, joyous crowd as the bride and the groom exchanged garlands, rejoicing the vibrant vista of his sole-interest.

Her slender form swayed effortlessly as Mrs. Chatterjee moved between people catering for them; her face, calm as her daughter encircled the fire with her groom.

With 'Anjali' (offering to the fire), the day's event culminated.

Finding Yash engaged with someone next to him, he slipped off. In the sea of faces, he turned and pushed, cruising through to get to her, who was now diminishing from his focus. A few grinning, snooping faces stared as he fought his way to the small room at the back, one he had never visited during his stay.

She was there, wrestling to lift what appeared like an over- loaded suitcase.

'Here...let me get it!'

Mrs. Chatterjee sprang back at her unexpected company. She had gone there to put some last minute items into one of Avni's luggage, in case she forgot in the pandemonium around. She had seen him in the *pandal,* taking pleasure in the admiring young gazes. She never expected him to gait behind her.

She stepped aside instructing him to shift it next to four others of the same kind.

'Thank you!'

Her coarse broken throat alerted him. He observed her eyes. They were swollen.

'Shall I get you something to eat or drink?'

She shook her head in denial. She was fasting since morning as per the tradition.

'I thought you might not turn up even today.'

His soul quenched. He received what he came seeking. She had missed him as he did.

'How couldn't I! I can never abandon your words....You know.'

His words projected command; a control on her thoughts as though she was obliged to think in accordance.

She wanted to revolt. But couldn't. His tone was but pleading and polite not authoritative. She acknowledged.

He registered her unspoken admission, maintaining the elegance of silence bridging the space in between.

It was a disturbing stillness that began enveloping, closing him on her, aggravating her anxiety.

'I'll...miss her!'

She said to erect a wall of letters for refuge, to keep him from consuming her.

'Well, in that case, keep Raktim here.....Instead of giving Avni away!'

Mrs. Chatterjee's face contorted for a moment, then cracked out into a light laughter, reading his rag.

'You talk too much!'

Shubham's face lit up. Those words sounded magical; special to him as though to have a meaning only he could perceive. He didn't feel embarrassed like a school boy but like a man, teased in love.

The whole world was fogged. The only visible entity being that graceful woman in whom, he found peace.

Her tension found a vent in him. She had been strained psychologically and physically to the edge of breaking. His little jest extended her limit a bit further.

The next day was *'Bashi Biye'* (Stale marriage), when Avni was marked with vermilion. It was time for Mrs. Chatterjee to bless her daughter as she leaves for her new life. She cried praying for life to be kind to her daughter; not to put her to tests, unbearable; thrash her to situations she had suffered.

Or suffering!

Chapter 10

'Dada, can you do me a favour?'
     'Yes.'
     'Can you spare some time for Mrs. Chatterjee?'
     Calling her by her surname felt so obstructive that he almost stammered while uttering it. His brain was rejecting her title now.
     'How by meeting Mrs. Chatterjee....can I do a favour to you?'
     Yash's raised brows caught him and he swore realizing his mistake while playing with words.
     'I want you to help her.'
     Yash's stillness unnerved him.
     'She writes. Very well!'
     Yash's squinted eyes told him that his friend was racing his horses on a separate track.
     'Dada! She deserves at least one chance. Can you?'
     Shubham held on to his friend's vigilant gaze with tremendous effort.
     'I fail to understand you. She has a gang of people in her family to help her. Why are you so bothered?'
     'As a friend!'
     'Yeah!....I saw your friendship spilling inside that five by five room.....that day!'
     Struck, Shubham shifted in his chair, uncomfortably.

'And not just me. A whole crowd had seen and sensed those electrifying sparks flying across....in there!'

'I don't know that! We were just talking!'

Shubham's voice soared in pitch.

Offended, he couldn't keep calm. People had no business in his doings. It was his life; his lookout and only he held command over it. He had endured enough of that kind of public policing at a time when he had not been sufficiently strong to protest. He wasn't the same Shubham anymore. He won't succumb.

'Fine!' Retorted Yash. 'What is it that you want me to do for her?'

'She writes. Can you please check if she can be used anyway?'

'A job?'

Yash's brows reached his hairline this time.

'I don't know.....But she is good. I've read few of her writings.'

'OK. Bring her along. I'll see what can be done.....if at all she is worth!'

Yash went back into his work; a pile of papers on his desk.

'Dada. Can't we visit her?'

'Why?'

It called for a new level of debating to persuade Yash to come to terms with him. He was positive that if he proposed this idea to her, she would instantly reject, declaring it as immature and foolish. Her insecurity wasn't a secret to him. Even her own family didn't know about her passion. She had admitted that it was alone he, whom she had let into her secret world.

*   *   *

The guests had finally left, leaving the house barren and her, drained. The wedding had been successfully closed and she was there, alone in the big house to relish the quiet. She was relaxed, Avni was doing fine with Raktim in his home. Her daughter was not staying very far, but she knew that being a married woman now, straying out often won't be possible for her. She satisfied herself with her regular phone calls. She was happy that her carefree child had begun to shoulder responsibilities. She was thankful that her darling daughter was safe and secured in her marriage; unlike her.

Her foraging heart wasn't able to get over the enigma that had clouded her and was increasing in volume and mass with every passing day.

Sitting in front of the mirror, she peered into her reflection trying to read the face that was looking back. What was it that was holding; making her to deny the truth. She was a grown lady; had seen and lived through the ups and downs of life. Had experienced every aspect of a relationship. She wasn't a girl in her teens to be curious about the other gender. She was sleeping her nights with one. Then, what had been pushing her to believe that all, that was happening, was real.

He was young; much younger than her. Had been very humble to her, because he happened to be a gentle man; nothing more. Then why, every beat of her heart was singing his name. Her loyalty was bound to her husband and yet, she was in constant hope that he would surprise her in his usual way, to pacify her angst-ridden soul.

The door bell tweeted breaking her chain of thoughts. It was an odd time. Without reckoning, she jumped and ran out of the door of her room. A pair of voices, she could hear, stopped her from sprinting down. There was someone more with him. She composed herself and walked down the stairs in a controlled manner.

At the landing, Shubham stood watching her descend elegantly, conscious of Yash's observant eyes on him.

'Good afternoon. Hope we didn't disturb you!' Yash said.

'No.'

Wondering what her husband's boss's son was doing in her house with Shubham, she ushered them to sit while asking Kalki to prepare some tea.

'You know....he works for a magazine.'

Shubham started without wasting time.

Yash had been very reluctant and he didn't want the opportunity to slip off, fruitless.

As the purpose of their unplanned visit revealed on to her, she was flabbergasted. Fixed by Shubham's enthusiasm and faith in her, she found herself at complete loss of words. He was mild yet imposing; his signature style to woo her into; something, she was yet to invent a way to resist.

'You don't have to be so shy! Trust me.'

'But.....they are personal!'

'They are precious. And he is the right person to evaluate them.'

Not sure if she was doing it right, she went up to get her diary. Her covert self was to be examined and exploited to see if she stood up to the standard of all those who called themselves educated because they possessed University degrees. Her intellect was to be put to test to see if she was at par with the literate world. She was scared; she lacked the certificates that would have stated her as smart like the one who was waiting down there to invigilate. She was bashful; she didn't want to fail Shubham and his faith in her.

'Mrs. Chatterjee....I appreciate.' Yash said nodding his head while flipping through the pages. 'You are good! There is a friend of mine working for a *Bangla* magazine. I'll talk to him. I'll definitely try my best.'

He posted a smile to both, his friend and her.

Mrs. Chatterjee remained silent trying to fathom if he was just being polite or genuine.

'I'll get back to you in these days.'

Taking her leave, Yash accompanied by Shubham, walked over to the door.

She was furious and wanted Shubham to stay behind. She was tired of his logic-less surprise.

At the door, Shubham announced his stay inviting another severe look from his friend. He ignored. He knew she was agitated and he needed to be there to convince her his point of view.

'What was that Shubham! Do you even realize...You belittled me in front of Yash?

'No I didn't! In fact, he liked your work!'

'No. He was respecting your words! I thought.....I could trust you!'

'I just want to see you doing something for yourself! I want to see you happy!'

'I am happy!'

The boiling tension inside her exploded.

She almost screamed. What did he know about her happiness; her plight.

'I have a family. A nice...good life. Everything a woman could ask for.'

She defended her stand. She had to. She needed to assure herself more, of the truth in her words, than him.

A sharp pain seized her forehead, squeezing her eyes as she fought to keep them focused on him.

He stepped closer.

'Mrs. Chatterjee is happy. But not Mahua.'

His words, deep in tone and meaning, jammed her.

'Mrs. Chatterjee has a family. A good life. But Mahua? She has nothing, except those words written in that notebook. I am not here for Mrs. Chatterjee. I am here for Mahua. And I want to see her happy.'

She turned away from him. Her eyes were laden and she didn't trust them.

'I want Mahua to live the life she had once dreamt. I agree. Yash may have kept the honor of my words. But I know that man. If he said.... he will try. He will. I assure you. Please....don't ignore him when he comes back. I might not be here....but I will be glad if you keep my words.'

I might not be here!

She swirled to face him in an instant.

'You are leaving!'

'Yes. The deal is finalized. Just have few days.....And I'll be gone.'

Her grief battled to dribble out of her eyes. Her throat went dry and clogged.

'I'll keep in touch.' He pushed a smile. 'And....when I come next time and I am at your door....I hope you won't shut it on my face!'

But she didn't quite absorb his jest then.

How she wished he hadn't ever come at all!

*   *   *

'Mahua, get me a cup of coffee.'

Shoving off the blanket, she dragged herself out of the bed, slipped into her slippers and walked down into the kitchen. It was late and she was worn-out. Not physically but emotionally.

She pulled open the overhead cabin and took out the jar containing instant coffee granules. She spooned a heap full into a coffee mug, added sugar and few drops of water and began beating.

Shubham had so conveniently announced his depart. There had been not a trace of sorrow in his words.

Why should there be!

The concoction started to develop bubbles that multiplied into more. The mixture began to thicken, just like her mind. It was dense since he had turned in to extend his well-wishing for her. He didn't do anything out of the way, guided by some other form of emotion. It was merely a gesture of good-will similar to that shown to an acquaintance; can be termed care, at best.

Pouring hot milk into the mug, she cursed herself for being such an idiot. He was young. She had seen eyes ogling him the other day.

Why should he be interested in an old hag!

She was smelting like the hot coffee, fizzing up leathery to the brim. Every damn bit of anguish that she had been enduring was her own creation. He had been there on business, not to romance with an aunty. He had been always clear, the way he was that day while showing indifference towards her feelings.

And there she was, torn between want and responsibility; between Mahua and Mrs. Chatterjee. She was furious with herself. How easily had he ripped her into two and left them to meddle with each other. If only there was a method to punish her, she would have incurred it upon herself for being that insultingly naive.

She entered her bedroom where her husband sat enjoying some cheap television comedy program, adjusted with irritating fake automated background laughter.

'Your coffee.'

She handed him the mug and waited. He took the first sip and continued whooping with the machine, irrespective of her being there, standing, hoping for a word of approval for her effort.

She was Mrs. Chatterjee, not Mahua he had come searching.

Offended, she climbed on to the bed, into her world.

The television roared into another insufferable hooting fit. She closed her eyes, virtually pressing her mind to shut up.

If only there was a button somewhere to switch off the damn brain!

But, her brain refused to obey. It kept replaying every moment they had spent together in order to locate the reason behind the mess she was in.

'Have you put a sackful of sugar in it!'

Her husband's condemnation pin-pointed the answer she was scrapping her brain for.

Respect.

Shubham had showered her with revere, she didn't receive from her husband. His admiring words were the culprit. She had felt exceptional in his company. His eyes, as she had always seen, weighed her as invaluable.

A fresh shot of anger rushed through her yet again, at her folly. She had twisted simple words to translate into nonsense.

What was I expecting? That he would crawl at the door asking me to be a part of his life!

Muffling her eyes and ears, she turned towards a new direction.

What if he actually landed, asking her? Would she be able to walk out leaving everything and everyone behind?

She removed her arm and threw a glance at her husband.

Her racing brain suddenly came to a jerking halt. She could extract no useful element as an answer from her mental ore.

Pulling her blanket over her face, she was thankful that her mind had finally given up.

And there was no point fantasizing something, that insane.

*   *   *

Her welled up eyes floated in his view as he lay stretched across on his bed. He knew she would be upset but had no idea that it would affect her to that extent.

He had not been at ease for the rest of the day.

The day had been unusually busy. Shyamal had called him in the office to start off the preliminary process. The other party was ready to pay the whole amount at one go. A good news for him; the sooner the money was in his account, the better it would be. Then he was able to persuade both Yash and her; though had taken a gruesome effort, but he was contended that both fell in line. He had opted to break the news of his departure casually, knowingly. It wasn't the right time for serious promises, but he would visit her soon. Soon, when he had established his own studio; had owned a bigger and better house; had a regular source of income before he makes any commitment to her. For, he had a competitor this time; one, who wasn't easy to slay.

He was tortured by her look, but had restrained himself. He didn't want to be a failure this time; not with her. He didn't want Yash to lecture him again about being irresponsible and unable to handle relations.

Everything that he had planned so far was progressing perfectly, yet he was having an uncanny hammering of loss; as if something important was slipping away.

To deviate himself, he closed his eyes and imagined her in his life; in his house.

A strange vacuum sucked him in. His consciousness began skidding away.

She was there, standing by the door in a bright blue sari, quite similar to the first time he had seen her. Her hair was scattered on her back; her large, velvety, densely lashed eyes, pouring love. He jumped joyously towards her. She had left all, that was a binding to her, behind, to be a part of his life. What could be better?

As he started closing on to her, she began moving; sliding away.

Gradually, the house began shrinking; reducing into a small cubicle-like space. Suffocating and enclosed. He panicked. He was back in his old dream.

Why?

He looked around. The chamber was different from the earlier one. It had a hoard of machines, instruments fitted. He remembered. It was the same hospital room where his father had breathed last. The bed stood in the middle. His heart began sinking in. He stepped towards it.

It was empty. Just lay covered with a white sheet. A bomb exploded inside him. He began searching. He knew his father had to be there, somewhere. He kept looking feverishly but couldn't find him.

Sapped, he sat. Large drops of tears began pouring out.

He woke up next morning with sodden eyes and a heavy head. He felt hollow.

*   *   *

'How many days are you leaving for?'

'Around a week! Why?'

'Take me along.'

Mr. Chatterjee shrugged his shoulders at her in a 'seriously' kind of irritation.

Mrs. Chatterjee bent her head over the suitcase she was loading with her husband's clothes and other requirements. She had known that he would not like to be accompanied by her during his official tour, yet she had asked him. She wanted a break from the place; from the disturbing brain of hers. She wanted to prove to her own self that she was still uncorrupted; wanted to fortify and uphold the sanctity of her marriage.

Avni was in Europe with Raktim.

She had never been alone with her husband since their marriage. First, there were people from her in-law's family, constantly nagging behind and then, kids followed. Her relation had been laden with accountability from the day one of its origin. Never could it get time or space to prosper. She hoped that some lone time with her husband might amend the lapses; might bridge the distance between them; repair the shortfalls. Thought, it could be a likelihood to build anew that, what was missing; give the relation a fresh start.

'What if I join somewhere?'
'Join where? Some ladies club?'
Mr. Chatterjee squeezed his forehead.
'No. Work.'
What if she couldn't go with her husband, Mrs. Chatterjee decided to give it a start; reach out and open up. Bridge the gap.
'Work? Where would you work? Who would give you work? Highly qualified people are having a tough time in getting something decent for them!' He crocked out a laughter. 'Stay at home and do what you can. Better for you....and me!'
Humiliated, she cursed herself for inviting it on her.
She had been well aware about his discomfiture; public shame regarding her insufficient schooling, yet she had laid too much trust; all in the name of resurrecting the relation.

'Keep an eye on Joy!'
He said in his usual bossy way.
'Why?'
'Don't send him out on the thirty-first night. With Avni not there to keep vigilance on him.....I don't want any problem.'
'But why would there be a problem?'

'Mahua! When will you learn to listen to me?' He said stiffening his voice. 'If you can't...I'll ask him not to set his foot out. You have no idea what youngsters are up to in the name of celebration. I don't want him to make a fool of me yet again!'

'Why do you always treat him in that manner? He is growing up. He deserves respect!'

The strength in Mrs. Chatterjee's tone took not just her husband but even her, by surprise.

'He deserves to be trained! So that he doesn't spoil my good name!' He retorted. 'All my siblings are blessed with many sons! All you gave me is this one....weakling! Instead of launching at me....knock some sense in his head. If he fails this year.... God only knows....what I might do!'

Appalled, she watched him gait into the bathroom with no remote repentance on his words.

It was his decision that they would be complete with a daughter and a son.

Her ever complaining mother-in-law, who had been distraught at the birth of first child as a girl, had danced for many days in joy. Mr. Chatterjee too, had walked down the lane with his nose, high in air. But as Joy grew up, his pride began to crumple under the deficits of his son's personality. However, their stringent source of income had prevented him from desiring for more. But, as his economic condition improved, as his social status elevated, he forgot the reason underneath.

All he could see now was that, he had just one son and his only son was nothing like what he desired.

Chapter 11

The day was warm. The Sun shined bright in the azure sky; rays spraying out through the clouds comforting the chill, penetrating into the bones.

The world was ready to execute exuberating plans to mark the day, as memorable as the one that had gone the previous year or the one that will come the next year; plans, to rock into the new year on some dancing number in a disco or to freak the night out on streets, with the gang or to enjoy the company of friends and family in a grand hotel or to watch the show of magnificent fireworks on the tallest building of the world, or to drag into the new day of the new year by gluing oneself on to the television set and its stale, reprobate programs in new envelop.

It was thirty-first December, the day to make new resolutions; the customary list of do's and don'ts to tag along, for the rest of the year.

Shubham too resolved to keep away from her for these few days of his stay in Kolkata. Bearing up with her streaming eyes one more time would call for a stupendous determination that, he was afraid, might not be possible for him. And falling to her tears now, would sabotage everything. He had to maintain a little distance, till all is ready for her to be a part of him. Though, he was positive about staying in touch;

had designed to send her a bouquet or something to cheer her up, when he could get off from Yash.

His buddy had called to relate him of his intentions regarding the new year's eve, which happened to be exactly what Shubham had been expecting from him.

The ethnically curved brass handle-bar tapped on the door for the second time before he could hear the latch being pulled, to open it. Shubham looked into his watch. His friend was a prompt character but that was too early to be felicitated as punctuality. It was impatience, rare one to find in Yash.

'Sahib, someone has come to meet you.'

A stumpy, pot-bellied, fair complexioned man, most probably in his fifties, wearing a pearly white shirt with minute polka dots printed on it and a pair of navy blue trousers, was seated, inspecting the hall with his protruding eyes.

'Shubham! Good to see you my boy!'

He exclaimed loud in a choked-up type of voice.

Shubham smiled artificially trying to goggle the identity of that flowing informal warmth, in his search machine.

'You forgot me!'

Came in the next blow.

How could he say 'yes'.

'I am Prokash Mitra?' He paused. 'Niranjan's friend and co-worker?' He paused again. 'I called you when he was in the hospital. Met you there?'

'Yes!'

Damn!

Shubham cursed his poor memory and requested forgiveness before taking the adjacent chair.

'Not a problem! Not a problem!'

Small bits burst out of his mouth.

Shubham noticed that what he took for red polka dots were actually tiny spits of '*pan*', the man was chewing which splattered out to design his shirt as he spoke. His nose was a big chunk of flesh on his spherical face and he had brushed his hair carefully to cover the barren spot on the top of his skull.

'I saw the ad in the paper. All set to sell it off!'

Few more pieces flew out.

'Yeah!'

'Crazy man!'

'Sorry!'

'Was desperate to get the house. I was with him when he bought it.'

And it cleared. His guest was referring to his father.

'Do you mind telling me why are you selling this one? It's gorgeous! You don't get to see such constructions these days!'

He did mind.

'I am settled in Mysore. Don't want to keep any burden hanging behind.'

'Burden? Is that what you feel about your father's passion?' Shubham was slightly taken by his sudden burst of energy. 'Niranjan got the house so that he can pursue his dreams. Coming from a modest business family, with no support at all, he had acquired everything on his own. And you discard it as a burden!'

Shubham kept quiet. The man was referring to his father by name. He didn't want to exhibit insolence.

Thankfully, Ganesh walked in with refreshments to space out the heat.

'Wonderful man! Some called him genius! I say....genius is a very superficial word. Nullifies your efforts....Only refers to public acceptance. I call him hard-working! Relentlessly pursuing what he believed in!' He lifted one cup. 'Some called him fanatic. I say...they were correct!'

Some of the red juice escaped his mouth to fall into the cup from which his guest took a long, gurgling sip.

Divulged, Shubham reserved himself from picking his cup.

'To sustain in that highly competitive, constricted genre of semi-commercial, when the world was going frenzy with the commercial mainstream, required madness!'

Though maintaining silence in the want of a direction or motive of the conversation, Shubham was amazed at the ardor with which the man was describing his father.

'Otherwise, you tell me! How many do you see with a reputation half his reach? It was during his grey days, when I had suggested him to shift to commercial, he had said, *Prokash Babu, filming a semi-nude beauty, drenching in rain, in a flimsy sari, to make audience ooze out money from their pants, is not my cup of tea!*' He lifted his cup in a gesture imitating his father's words. '*If I was to just earn money, I would have been happy selling readymade garments at my father's shop and would have settled with Shipra, whose father was ready to compensate his daughter's weight, with a bag full of cash!*'

He laughed a heartfelt laughter. Shubham couldn't remain untouched. He smiled. The man had this unique quality of merging past with present, effortlessly. His narration related immaculate closeness to his father.

'Niranjan loved challenges! Traveling to new places for stories, then filming and screening them for a handful audiences, called for risk-taking caliber. When his film *'Upshagarer Pare'*(On The Shores, By The Bay) won him his first National Award, that he could finally get a strong footing.'

Shubham had not seen the film, but it was the one that had propitiously concealed the malicious talks relating to his mother's suicide bringing rest to his ears and fame to his father.

'A little peace was installed into his life after all that he had faced due to his wife!'

'Excuse me!'

Shubham reacted immediately. That man just blamed his mother; pushed everything so shamelessly on to her as though she had done all that consciously, purposefully.

His temper shot up.

'I had warned Niranjan many times...but he seemed to be possessed by her! It was due to her that he had to leave his family. People weren't this open minded then...you see. And what he gets in the end? Police interrogation on a murder charge! Outrageous! When he had always been trying to figure a way out to hold on to his wretched life!'

'I hope you know.....you are talking about my mother!'

'Yes! Mitra rejoined with equal strength. 'It was not a marriage! It was a mirage! A dissatisfying mirage that ripped Niranjan of all his happiness. If she was so sensitive, she should not have come along with him at all! He didn't force her. She chose him! He was her ex-husband's friend and couldn't see her going through all that hardships of widowhood!'

Prokash Mitra's words fell like balls of fire from Hell, burning him. That man was lying, biased to his father. How could this outsider be true when he himself had seen his mother suffering all along while his father remained unaffected.

'Otherwise...you think! How is it that he soared heights just after she left! Because he was relieved.'

'That's enough! I am not listening to all this bullshit!' Shubham sprang to his feet. 'I am very busy. I don't have time to waste!'

The man did the same.

'Shubham! You just resemble Niranjan. You remind me more of that uncle of yours!'

Shubham stopped immediately.

'You know Nilikanta Thakur?'

'I don't know his name. But I have known no bigger brute than him! I am sorry if it hurts!'

The mockery in his tone didn't bother Shubham. He was more interested in the label attributed to his legal rival.

'How do you know him?'

'He and his cronies had stormed into our office and broke a camera. Stupid! If he knew how much that costed!'

'But why? When?'

'Well, I don't know the exact cause. I had rushed in along with others when we heard that loud crash. He had been shouting at your father. Called him all sorts of names!Swore like I have heard no one before! Barked...that Niranjan went sniffing wealth behind a widow! How insulting! That too... in front of the whole staff! It was your father, who didn't let down his honour. I wanted to call the police...but he stopped me!'

'When did this happen?'

'I don't remember the date. But as if...the brother and his vicious insinuations weren't enough....the sister decides to slit her wrists the next morning!'

Shubham collapsed into the chair.

Everything became as clear as crystal. His father had been livid due to Nilikanta and took it out on his mother. His poor mother was put to an end because her husband couldn't handle his brother-in-law. The wild, ill-reputed, rebellious love story had fallen a prey to immature handling of emotions.

Prokash Mitra sat by his side and patted him on his arm.

'Son....I didn't come here to trouble you. There is something very important I came to discuss with you.'

Shubham didn't react.

A polythene bag with bold imprint stating **Ananda Bhandar,** with address written in smaller size was kept on the table. Prokash Mitra lifted it and pulled out a silver file.

'This is what I came here for.'

Saying, he placed it on Shubham's lap.

Shubham unfolded the cover. Inside, in bold letters were written,

SHUKNO PATA (Dried leaf)
By:
Niranjan Sarkar.

'Your father's last work! It was with me when he met with that fatal accident. We were about to start working on it.'

'Thank you.'

Flummoxed, he couldn't find anything else to say. The man kept the work with him for almost three years only to return it back and that dramatically! He didn't know how to judge him; fool or faithful.

He had known that his father had been preparing to work on an important project then, with a reputed international channel on some socio-cultural topic and had been away for many months regarding it. He had not investigated into details. He was happy, his father had not been around to comment on his association with his boss.

It was the same time he had been busy with Mereline's exhibition which ultimately blew off, like his relation.

'No! You don't understand. This is a masterpiece. Go through it. It needs to be shot!'

'Ok. Then shoot it!'

Shubham placed it back on the table and closed the file.

'This is preposterous!'

Big chunks of his buccal debris flew out on to Shubham's face. He wiped them while trying to get what caused Mitra to yell that way.

'I have been preserving it for last three years. If I had to make it....I wouldn't have waited this long! But I cannot. This is Niranjan's baby. His hard-work. I cannot take it from him. I cannot earn fame by stabbing my friend on his back! I may not be doing well...but I am not a cheat!'

'Then what do you want me to do?'

Still vague at his intension, Shubham clasped his hands against his lips.

'It can be our scoop! We can make it together. This way....neither will I be cheating on him nor can anybody point a finger towards me. Many of the staff members think I had deliberately kept it so that I can lick the cream off his milk! It is just that I couldn't trace you...to hand it over.

When I saw the ad...I contacted the property dealers and found out about you.'

Shubham could not deny his point. He had avoided from coming back for these few years. He had changed jobs and places like a nomad but didn't return. Just couldn't.

'See...I am not a film maker. I am a photographer.'

'I am there! You just need to be there with me so that the crew doesn't feel otherwise. You see...it was a much talked about project. And Niranjan's death immortalized it. Almost all old folks know about it.'

So that kept him from making it!

'Well...I cannot be with you. I have other plans.'

'Then....let's do it on papers. Proper agreement. Then.... it will be mine. No one can question me.'

Shubham didn't know how to get it over. He had no intention to get involved, at the same time, giving it away didn't feel good either.

'Ok. I'll see what I can do.'

The man took out a card and handed it to him.

'My number.' He said pointing at an array of numerals on the card below his name. 'Call me. I'll be waiting.'

And displayed a broad sticky smile that of a sales representative trying to persuade the customer into agreeing upon a deal.

*   *   *

'Not shrewd. Desperate!'

Yash finally spoke after being hushed by the taunt from that hostile waitress who took offense when he had expressed his interest to know about the newly set pub more than her bare legs.

Kolkata or Calcutta; a historic cocktail; a magical mixture of graceful, age-old Bengali culture and modern style; traditional and bold. Its archaic monumental buildings pronouncing grandeur of the bygone days while its sleek modern architectural glamour, flaunted progress at par with the rest of the world. The roadsides were crammed with malls, cafes, pubs, shops, glittering in the dark night of the eve. *Phuchkawalas, chatwalas,* small food-stalls, all crowded the streets with rickshaws, cars, taxis, buses, making Shubham feel strangely at home.

'We don't serve Yellow pages, uncle!' She had said batting her eyelids, sarcastically, reducing Yash's enthusiasm to dust.

'All he wants is an NOC!'
'On the contrary, I think you should give it a go. Try it out.'
'Dada! Get real! It is not my job.'
'There is always a first time!'
Shubham looked away. His friend was sounding persistent like his father who had been very particular that he should learn violin in spite of his repeated refutations.

At times, he felt that Monalisa had been more real than his violin, to his father; had been interested in her all along and wanted to lay his hands on her, so arranged the lessons. This idea jeered at him even more reducing him to nothing; like a tissue paper; use and throw type. He still remembered the coldness in his father's eyes when he had screamed his pain out, after flinging that violin at him.

'You betrayed Ma. You fought with her and killed her because you wanted to be with other women!'

'No. Monalisa is nobody.'

'She is a whore! But you! How I wish you were dead instead!'

His father had walked out without speaking anymore. After that, they had never really spoken much except for important issues like payment of fees; air fare; dates of arrivals and departures, which he used to plan carefully so that they had minimum time of contact. His relation with Mereline did invite few concerns and advices from his father but he had kept him from poking in much.

A pleasant looking waitress came in to place their order on the oval, high steel-table, standing on a steel stalk with a round foothold at the base. They were seated inside an open cubicle from where he could see the mob being driven crazy by the DJ on the floor.

'What have you decided about the case?'
Yash asked while tipping their glasses with the drink.
That was another issue Shubham was yet to look into. Prokash Mitra's account reiterated Dasgupta's portrait of Nilikanta. He knew that he needed a strong, experienced lawyer to handle his case and asking Dasgupta would mean to abide by his clause. But it was his mother's property and he somehow wasn't ready to give it off, even in exchange for good money. Simultaneously, he knew he didn't have much time.
'Nothing!'
Yash filled their glasses with another pour of the light brown coloured drink.

'Shubham, keeping the property would mean a lifelong tussle with Nilikanta. And that is what Mr. Sarkar wanted to bar!'

Mr. Sarkar wanted to mend his frayed ego!

He took one sip after another driving the sour liquid into his system. It felt sweeter against his bitter heart.

What was the logic behind returning it after her death, he didn't understand. If it had been with him, such situation wouldn't have arrived. In these years, Nilikanta too would have realized and come to terms with him.

'Did you manage to get something for Mrs. Chatterjee?'

How he wished to address her by her name.

'I called her. She said she would let me know.'

'I hope!'

Shubahm sighed. It was very important that she steps out of her house; her set confines. The sooner she gets unconstrained, the easier it would be to cut her off from her old life.

Yash refilled third time.

'What is it...that is in your head?' Yash asked promptly. 'If I know you well...there is something cooking in there! Shubham why? Why are you doing this? She has a family! Respect in the society! Two kids. One married recently! Do you realize...how many lives are at stake?'

Shubham didn't refute or retort. He was au fait about the gravity of the consequence.

He drank half his goblet, in a gulp.

'I don't understand one thing.' Yash began to stammer. '*Tui saala ekti khachchar*(You are a jerk)*!*' Shubham drew his strong eyes on his friend. 'But she? She is so... matured!'

His friend was now dragging. 'Then how on earth.......she could fall for you?'

'Dada, when you can't handle.....then why do you drink!'

His friend was slurring his words; struggling to maintain the sync between his brain and his vocal muscles.

'When you cannot handle......then why...do you go for older ladies?'

Yash was now dripping towards the direction, Shubham hated most. The normal, well-adaptive, good mannered Yash had a history of transforming into a misproportioned character, when drunk, grumbling abusively to begin with followed by an episode of wallowing in self-pity.

Shubham knew that the night had just begun.

'Do you know.....how much Mereline was hurt? Tell me....how do you plan to leave Mrs. Chatterjee....after you are done with her?'

Shubham took few more sips. He needed strength to endure.

'Dada....Do you want me to go?'

'No! No!' He drank from his glass. 'But.....she....is homely-type! She'll be destroyed!'

'I am not destroying anyone! She doesn't know anything. I haven't told her yet.'

'Then don't!.....Go!....Go and get to work. Set up your studio. Don't even piss.....in the direction of her house!'

Shubahm waited patiently for his pal to slip into the next level.

'I know......you miss your mother. But you......cannot sleep with moms....to be a man!'

Shubham removed his eyes to look outside through the glass wall. The place was bustling with people and traffic.

His friend, philosopher and guide was now completely off-trail of what he was jabbering. And there was no sense in trying to make him realize. He was well versed in that matter.

Yash would drink till his wit and his wallet, both go empty. Worst, he ostracized to be interrupted.

Just then, Yash slammed his glass on to the table and started unconsciously murmuring about how his father thought him to be a good-for-nothing; how his mother had been hunting for a bride of her choice, in case, he might carry a hippy home someday; how the girl he had been fishing for so long, got hooked to his rascal cousin; how his boss was tormenting him as he didn't take her out on a date and on and on.

Shubham was glad, his pal was in his second phase. It was just a matter of time, when his buddy would pass out and would be much more civilized to handle.

After all, everyone has his own style to take out his pent-up wastes!

It was five past eleven, when his cell buzzed, showing an unknown number.

'Please.....help me...Dada!'

Shubham jumped to his feet. Though the voice was flickering and the background, noisy, he still could recognize it well.

'Joy! What's wrong?'

The mob had gone wild. The music was deafening. What he received from the other end was too poor to gauge. So, he walked straight into the toilet hoping for some audibility. But it wasn't free either. Blocked with repugnant smell, the place was swarming with couples engrossed in what they considered prohibited outside.

'Joy.....where are you?'

Luckily, he could grab a gratis corner.

Shubham dashed into the cubicle to find Yash drinking. Pulling out a lum-sum amount, he pinned it down under a bottle.

'What...happened?'

Yash asked at his haste, sluggishly.

'We have to go. Now!'

'No! I am not finished!'

'You can finish later. Now we have to go!'

Grabbing his hand, he tried to pull Yash up, who jerked him away impulsively.

Shubham knew he was on for a tough challenge. Without reacting, he seized his arm tightly and towed a stiff-legged, swaying, barely-balanced Yash through the crowd, solely with the power of mind rather than muscle. Bumping into a dancing couple, knocking a waitress, tossing few glasses shattering on to the floor, he could finally pull his drunk dude out in the chill.

The cold helped. Yash shook his head vigorously.

'What's that....Urgency?' He bawled.

'Give me the keys, Dada. We have to go to the police station.'

'Why?'

He was still yelling and shaking.

'Because Joy is in there.'

'Who...Joy?'

'Joy Chatterjee. Mr. Chatterjee's son.'

He found saying Mr. Chatterjee far more preferable.

'So?'

'We have to go and get him!'

'Why we? He is his....father's headache!'

'His father is not in town!'

'That's not...my problem!'

'It's my problem!' Shubham shouted. 'I cannot let her go to the police station! Now, give me the keys, will you?'

He had been putting up with that absurdity since the whole evening. He was tired.

Yash reconciled.

The front of the pub was comparatively less illuminated than the main street.

Out of the dim, emerged a figure with numerous silver chains glittering on the chest. Taller than Shubham, he treaded up to him and grabbed him by his collar.

'What boss!' He spoke in a coarse tone. 'Why are you barking?'

Shubham's slack temper broke all bounds.

Shoving the hand off, he pushed the man hard to hurl him back few steps.

Instantly, two more figures surfaced from the dark. All attired in black jackets, tight jeans and dangling silvers around their neck and fingers. All three surrounded him, similar to that of a cackle of hyenas, circling their prey before attack.

'Easy boss! Easy!' Yash jumped in and placed a hand on the chest of one of them. 'We are going. Sorry! Easy!'

Covering Shubham partly with his body, eyeing their move, he suspended both of his hands in air in surrender. Neither was his tongue slurring nor were his feet, staggering. He appeared to be in total alertness.

The gang exchanged few glances between them, punched Shubham hard on his chest and pointing warning fingers, receded back into the shadow.

Yash pressed his palms against his face. Shubham knew why. They could have landed into grave danger if Yash had not acted in time.

Without any word, Yash marched ahead towards, where his car waited in parking. Shubham followed.

The car roared on to the road. Tuning in the radio, Yash twisted the knob increasing the volume probably to create a barrier between them.

His favourite RJ was on air.

The lanes were flooded with vehicles. Shubham held tight to his seat as Yash swayed the four wheels from one lane to the other, banging the horn in frustration; honking long and loud.

The car took a sharp right turn, almost throwing Shubham out, when the countdown began.

'9....8...7'

The car zoomed into a darker bye lane to its left.

'6...5..'

The car bumped on to the main road again and swept passed two stylish saloons on the right.

'4...3.'

It took a sharp U-turn around the divider.

'2.'

And slewed for a while before thudding onto the road again.

'1'

Yash pressed the breaks. The car screeched to a halt, throwing Shubham forward, hitting on to the dashboard.

'Happy New Year!' The RJ screamed. *'Welcome to the year...'*

Yash turned off the ignition, jumped out, slammed the door behind and tramped off to run up the stairs on the right side of the road.

Shubham tracked behind.

The police-station was an old, single-storey building with slatted roof. He wondered if they constructed each one with the same lay out.

The stairs entered into a corridor, which took him to the inner office, on the left and lock-ups, on the right.

The place was comparatively crowded than the last time, in his memory. Cells were filled with boys and girls; mostly well-dressed, either negotiating with the men through the bars or huddled at a corner, waiting with puffed eyes, scanning the crowd for known faces.

One such eye caught him and he pushed through.

'Shubham da!'

Joy screeched in a cracked voice.

A blast of pungent smell plunged his nostrils.

'Take me out.... Please!'

Joy spoke, slightly dragging, one word into another.

'He is drunk!'

Yash commented with his hands planted on his hips, in disgust.

Shubham didn't dare to remind him of his own condition just a few minutes previously.

'No *saar* (sir)! Not possible. Caught totally out! Driving at 100. You should be happy, he didn't run over anybody!'

The constable they approached for help was from the adjoining state with a typical accent about his language.

'But he is just a kid.'

'Everyone is. See.' He said pointing towards the jails. 'All toads of the same pond! Come day after tomorrow.'

After mulling over for some time, Yash approached the *hawaldar* again; his face and body showing desperate tactics to win the man over who was in his forties, wearing a murky uniform; his protruding stomach dissected into two by his belt and was shaking his head in disagreement.

Shubham selected to stay with Joy who was all red and white, out of fear, very much like him when he had been summoned, nine years back.

'Where were you when she died?'
'Sleeping in my room.'
'Was your father at home?'
'No.'
'Did you see or hear anything suspicious in the house or around?'
'No.'
'Do you doubt anyone or anything?'
'No.'
'How was the relation between your parents? Did they fight often?'
'No.'

He had been nervous. He had lied. He wanted to escape.

After lasting for what felt like an eternity outside the police station as instructed by the constable, the man handed Joy over to them in exchange for a bundle full of crisp notes.

Hoisting Joy who was still limp on legs, the two headed towards the car.

Chapter 12

'Shall I wait?'

'No. I'll walk home.'

It was forty minutes past one, when the car reached in front of the Chatterjee's dwelling.

Shubham clicked the door open and stepped out. Then he pulled out a flaccid Joy.

'Dada. Happy new year!' He bent down to peep through the window.

Yash smiled.

'Take care. Shall call you tomorrow...Arrey! Today, later.'

No matter how intolerable the man got after raining his inside with alcohol, Shubham still loved him. That man had kept him strong when he had laid his father on pyre and set him ablaze.

When the world was ecstatically welcoming the new year, that man was running from table to table in a pathetic police station, just for him.

*   *   *

The wall clock was taunting her, sneering at her for over-ruling her husband's words. It was haunting her by ticking away into the depth of the night. She wanted it to stop and

164

tell her that she was panicking for no good reason; that there was still time for him to return; that he wasn't picking her calls because he was only a few steps away from the door.

The door-bell tweeted, drumming into her heart. She ran and unbolted the heavy door in no time and pulled it apart to come face to face with not her son, but her incalculable visitor who had never failed to elude her. She had received a grand collection of roses that evening from him wishing her a "Refreshing New Year". She had been scratching to decode the meaning ever since. And there he was, standing at the door, fuming in alcohol. She swallowed; her heart missed a beat; her brain searching for words.

Her palpable ill-at-ease caused Shubham to step aside and reveal his reason for violating his resolution on its very first day.

The sight of her son cowering from behind Shubham, though confusing, relieved her. She stepped aside to let them in, expecting an explanation for them being together. But when nothing of the sort came from any of the men, she opened her mouth to ask. But fell back, at once, witnessing the wretched condition of her son.

Unsteady, his feet were striving hard to hold on to the floor. Not just that. He was smelling awfully foul; his red eyes, bulging out like those of a toad.

'What's wrong?'

She stepped closer. The strong stink pierced through her olfactory organs, hitting her brain.

Her son was blitzed!

'You are drunk!'

Joy bowed his head down,burrowing it into his chest.

'Answer me!'

She grabbed him by the collar and shook him vigorously.

He didn't utter a word. Just fluttered like a leaf.

She turned the entire strength of her eyes on to Shubham.

Jittered, he licked his dry lips. She was furious and awaiting an explanation. Choosing his words carefully, he began.

No near could he get to completion that she terminated it with a tight, smashing slap across Joy's face, waking him up from drooping.

Shubham chewed in the remaining of his words.

'You promised!'

Her voice died, choked by the lump in her throat.

'I am sorry Ma!'

A dry, apathetical apology burped out making her step backward in repulsion.

Clasping her head in her hands, she sank into a chair next to her in dismay.

Taking the opportunity, Joy began stomping up the stairs, balancing his unsteady feet by holding on to the hand rails.

She watched ruefully as her sozzled trust stumbled bit by bit to hide in the dark. If only she could take refuge in some unseen corner somewhere. How was she to explain all that to her husband; how was she to justify her faith in her child. If a mother couldn't trust her womb, whom was she to trust more?

Shubham watched her shaking her head violently from side to side. He knew what was she anticipating. Drawing a chair, he sat close to her.

Taking one of her hand, he bent his head down to her ears and whispered.

'Don't worry! Mr. Chatterjee would never come to know. Everything had been taken care of.'

Alert, she uncurled. His warm skin was caressing hers; his knees brushing against hers. His nearness unnerved her.

'I know you are scared. But you don't have to be!'

She studied him.

It was the same face she had adored; the same set of eyes with the boyish touch. The same man she had trusted all the time since they had met. And he was sitting there comforting her.

And she wanted to believe him.

It wasn't the first time, they were alone together. They had spent hours in the privacy of a deserted, secluded terrace of an empty house; had read, discussed, debated, argued but never had it been so abstract to her, so dreamlike, as if she was visualizing him the way she had often done without realizing, only to pull herself back to the truth and be hurt.

A stiff whiff of spirit entered her nose rationalizing her brain. It was time, she should get hold of herself and get real.

She drew her hand out from his grip.

It irked him.

'You don't have to reason out anything to anyone. This will stay just between you and me. No one will ever know. I am glad Mr. Chatterjee isn't here. Otherwise'

'Otherwise nothing of the sort would have happened!'

Cutting him, she pulled herself out, from the chair, from his proximity, from his distracting effect.

She felt unclean. Shubham's words insulted her, as if they were not addressing to Joy's condition but were suggesting to contain something clandestine; illicit between them. As if he was referring to the dirt hidden in the depth of her heart; was striping her naked off her unblemished outer cast, off her sham mask of purity; exposing her sinister, her filth.

Guilt surged hitting her and she sauntered few feet away from him.

'This is all my fault. If Mr. Chatterjee was here, he wouldn't have let him out. It has to be properly dealt with!' She spoke tightly, emphasizing the actuality on herself, curbing her brain from drifting. 'He needs to be told!'

Shubham's mouth fell open. He was more than surprised; he was offended. She seemed to overlook his efforts; disrespect his advice. He had taken all that pain simply to keep her safe from Mr. Chatterjee and his wrath. Yet she seemed not to register; rather inflexible about ruining it all. It began charging him, flexing his patience. Moreover, her abrupt desertion from his cuddling intimacy, rebuffed him.

'Why do you want trouble?' He jostled the chair off and galloped to her side. 'He will rip you before laying his hands on Joy! Do you think he will be interested in a situation where his son was driving someone else's car without a license and that too drunk! No.' He bawled. 'He'll not spare him for landing up in jail. Neither you!' His scarlet eyes, pinning her; piercing into her.

She raked him alarmed at the level of his accuracy at picturing her husband.

'All he cares is his name! But still if you think that he needs to know then let Joy tell him. He is not that naive! He knew whom to reach out for, even when out of senses!'

The sheer force of his tearing voice, threatened her and she stepped back. He closed up, almost touching her.

'Just keep quiet. Let him shoulder his mistake. Only then will he be cautious next time. You don't get in! Let them deal.'

'No! This is my son you are talking about! And I'll have to make sure that there is no next time. This is my family and I cannot keep quiet. My husband deserves to know... And my son needs me!'

She dissented raising her voice to match his. But she had to. He was ordering her; telling her to step aside in her own family.

How could he?

After weakening her by halving her into two, he was now trying to stub her off her only support; her family. Why, she didn't know. He had already done enough damage. She couldn't allow more.

Joy was in her custody; was her liability. Her husband had warned her yet, she had given in to Joy's pestering. She had to bear up with whatever was in store for her. She had no choice.

My family, my husband, my son!

Smacked, he backed a few steps, fixated to her face; her exotically moulded face. The face he had been so much stuck on to. Nevertheless still beautiful, it appeared alien; farfetched from the one he had claimed in his dreams. The one that had flushed at his presence, reacted to his words.

Her finely lined, kohl eyes too, were not sparkling as they always did when set on him. They were cold, stoned like those of his mothers', when she had laid spread on the bed that morning.

He panicked; she was slipping away.

'Your son, your husband, your family! Then what about us? What about all that, that we have been living since all these days!'

The truth came thundering down on her. All that, was not her imagination; not fiction, but fact.

Her eyes shot wide; her heartbeat escalating to a deafening speed. Her brain stopped.

She was not alone in it. He was as much into it as she was. Her body untied; loosened. It was all real. He was crying out his confession; demanding her union. Her eyes lost its rigidity. She rooted.

'I have tolerated enough! Have suffered...waited enough! I cannot share you anymore with anyone!'

His voice echoed inside her like a tune resonating in a hollow tube; settling deep within her, filling her.

'I want you. Come with me, to my world. I care for nothing more...only you to make me happy. Be mine!'

She shut her eyes tight. He had come to her, claiming her. But, at a very unfortunate time.

The time demanded her judgment. The time demanded justice.

'This is my world! Go away Shubham, and never return.'

Mrs. Chatterjee shattered. Tears rushed to build up behind, pressurizing her eyes.

'What!'

Hit, he rebounded, demanding an explanation for her incongruous behaviour. But stern, she held her ground, uncompromising. Her eyes pained as she maintained them fixed on a distraught, hysterical Shubham; not-bating, non-streaming, counteracting his animosity with every drop of valor she could pull together.

Then who am I to you, he had screamed, mad at her iciness.

A good friend, was all she could offer him, before scuttling up the steps without looking back.

*   *   *

The floodgates of her heart had been blasted to bits by his acknowledgment. Tears streamed down her face as soon as she turned away from him. She didn't look back, afraid to show them to him. The test had been more audacious than she had foreseen. With every ascending step, her heart was pulling her to turn and run down to him in acceptance; in obedience; in commitment, binding herself to him.

Once inside her room, she bolted the door, frightened that he would follow. He had been wild in anger when she left him and her heart kept knocking, telling her that he would try breaking in. And if he did so, she would be left with no cover, no strength to feign any further. She would have to resign to him; to his want, his claim. She wasn't able to think clear; her brain fogged with a jumbled dust of emotions.

A part of her wanted him to chase her down, to prove in action his longing; his binding to her, while the other part objected claiming that she was a woman of dignity and could under no circumstance, fall beneath her status. As one half of her brain cursed her for shooing him off and was mourning at the loss of her love, the other half debated logic; that she was not just a woman but a mother. While one side of her soul craved for the reverence he had graced her with, the other side eschewed her, predicting and projecting the slanders and ill-repute she would earn not just from strangers but from her own dear ones, especially her children.

Where Mahua wanted him to embrace her in the asylum of his arms, comforting her with his love, Mrs. Chatterjee warned her reminding that she was a married woman. Her body was betrothed to her husband and desiring something of the kind was a transgression. A sin.

Divided, she waited. Her eyes, her ears, her heart; all her senses in attention for the thrust; the burst that will break down the meek barrier between them. She waited for the moment, when she would bow down to her love with the excuse that she was left with no choice; when she would live with the excitement of being hunted down by desperate desire and not just owned to satisfy mere requirements; but claimed with respect and love, together.

But, nothing happened.

Her tears dried on her rosy cheeks, her ears numb in the encompassing silence, her heart slack in her chest. He didn't come. He was gone, forever.

A fresh gush of hot, smelting saline trailed down. It was all over. No one would be there to cheer her up; to praise her; to make her feel worthy. No one would care if she was happy or sad; if she was lonely and needed someone to talk.

There would be no one to tease or laugh with her; to abide and submit to her.

She wiped her tears again and again trying to come to terms with the reality. After all, it was her decision. A choice, she had made. It was just a few days before, when she had found herself blank when addressed with the situation, in her mind. Tonight, amidst all that chaos, she got her answer.

She was Mrs. Chatterjee, a dutiful wife, a responsible mother.

Her children needed her. Her daughter was recently married and she couldn't jeopardize her life, meagerly for excitement. Her son was in trouble and she couldn't dump him to perish in the morbid dark of intoxicating dungeon, to elevate someone else's spirits.

Her husband may not have showered her with beautiful words but had been loyal to her and she couldn't cause him shame.

Mahua was long dead, buried under the weight of the title she adorned. What Shubham excavated was a carcass; an evidence of once-existing, dreaming, hopeful life that had been squashed, ossified by fate.

She was Mrs. Chatterjee and would continue to be Mrs. Chatterjee; her only identity, her destiny.

She couldn't blame Shubham for being aggressive, demanding; couldn't tag him as licentious for laying bare his yearning heart.

Everything that begins, has an aim, a destination. The objective of love is relationship; total surrender in mind and body.

Lack of emotional arousal in her relation with her husband, qualified her superficial involvement with Shubham, as consoling. But, such a platonic attachment was hard to comprehend, especially for a young, enthusiastic man like him.

Barely enough a woman she was, when her trembling body had been torn into by her stout husband showing no mercy. She had screamed and cried in pain, alone, within herself, scared and ashamed to let it out to the world. It was not love that she had been subjected to but torture. And it repeated over and over again. In few days, she neither feared nor desired it, but had accepted it as a duty of a wife to her husband like many others she had been performing, ever since.

In the seclusion of her room, she accepted another secret that she had been averting since all these days. She had attributed it to her advancing age and had been planning to see her doctor regarding it.

It was that day when Shubham had sat sharing tea with her in her small kitchen after his return from Banipur that she had experienced it, at the very outset. She had gone wet, spontaneously; involuntarily. And it had frequented every time they had been together. Although, she kept telling herself that it was some kind of body malfunctioning that needed medical help.

But that night, she, with all her experience, sat cursing for letting herself loose.

Rubbing her sore skin off the dampness, she blamed herself for encouraging him. If only she had not drifted along blind in her quest for recognition, approbation, nothing of the kind would have taken place. She was due this punishment. He was gone and for good. Soon, he would forget her and be fine with his life.

She sighed deep and long. Dragging herself off the bed, she pushed the door open and crossed the empty verandah, dead in silence and entered her son's room.

Joy was sleeping, spread in his dirty clothes on his bed, still stinking strong of spirit. She sat next to him caressing his face, head, neck and back.

She knew the reason behind Joy's outrageous upheaval. Her child needed special care; was in want of respect, just like her.

*   *   *

The Ellora Path bye-lane was a dwelling for the privileged in the area. Half past two in the morning was too late for lights to glitter inside the marvelously masoned houses that lined the either side of the street. But that night was different. It was New Year; a new morning and the lucky ones felt obliged to welcome it with a bang. Most of the residences had their curtains pulled to reveal sparkling chandeliers and jubilant faces, gleaming through the glass windows. The road was spawning with automobiles of various colour, brand and style.

Shubham sprinted out on to the street after banging the iron gate behind and almost bumped onto someone, a lady, waiting in the dark, obscure due to scanty light and mist in his eyes.

'Sorry,' he barked without care and jogged on. People crammed the boulevard, wishing and bidding merry 'goodbyes', with blissful promises of reunion.

Quick-footedly, he crossed the area and took the first right and entered a relatively quieter zone.

Kicking pebbles, his silent silhouette staggered under the orange glow from the lamp posts in absolute solitude.

Once again he was hurt; his hopes had been smashed; his feelings, teased and tortured.

His mother chose to die for his father than to live for him; Monalisa had kissed him and made love to his father. Mereline had slept with him and dreamt of great fascinating career. There had always been something more important than him. His father had paid his bills but had never spent time with him. He had his films to fill him.

And she...

Shubham stopped abruptly whooshing out a blast of dust in the air from the tip of his shoes.

She caused him more trauma than any of the others. He had respected her, trusted her, admired her for her qualities. She was his Guardian Angel who had appeased him both, in his dreams and days. Made him feel like a man.

He had desired to preserve her, to lush her with liberty, with independence that he had so often witnessed in her ways; read in her lines.

But her family, her son, her husband claimed the front seat; the lead, pushing him back. She chose her closed frontiers against the bracket-less world he wished to show her.

When she had marched up thwarting him, he had a strong maddening drive to break in, seize her and force her to submit to him; tell her that he wasn't a toy to be pushed to the corner when done with the game. Where was that sincere wife or that obligate family person when she was blushing under his gaze or responding to his touch.

But he could not do it.

Swallowing his grudge, exercising miraculous control, he had managed to tow himself out of the house.

His feet picked up again and took few turns, right and left before entering into the Sunflower Path.

He noticed that the Chief Justice's abode had vehicles parked on the either side of the outer wall in a line, declaring that the party was far from over.

Crossing the array of cars, he approached his house jeering at himself. It was all over for him. She had written him off as a 'good friend'.

And the house..

He stopped to look up at the large red-brick structure, shabby with its overflowing mass of wild vines.

It would be gone too, practically that very morning. He sighed.

Taking out the long, saw-jawed key from his pocket, he flung the door open. An echoing silence welcomed him. It was gloomy, deep blue under the dim light from the night bulb. He walked in. His footsteps resounded, proclaiming the singularity of his existence. He had released Ganesh and his wife as their services would no longer be required.

A line of stuffed and sellotaped boxes were pushed by one of the walls. The view increased the tightness he already felt in his chest. In a matter of few hours, he would be uprooted from his soil. The thought sank deep in his soul. A void rapt him in. Everything became pointless. His life, his hopes, his expectations; everything. He felt like a parched, detached leaf, wandering with the wind clueless of its course.

A silver shining on the table, luminescent like a glow-worm in the dark, caught his bemused eyes and he picked it up. It was his father's manuscript.

He peeped into his watch. It showed five minutes to three. The day would break in an hour or so. The black would be won over by colours brightening the days of millions across the globe; to enrich many with hope; to motivate many more to take a step further and discover a new world, they have never explored; to push one last time, to seek out a new horizon.

For him, it would bring an end to his reason to be home; to be in the city- the City of Joy.

Sleep was far from him and instead of tossing and turning on bed, he opted to spend the remaining part of the night with the file. A cruel, sardonic smile stretched across his face. In that hour of loss and despondency, his only companion happened to be the vestiges of the man, he had nurtured least interest in, when alive.

Walking into his room, switching on the lights, changing into a pair of clean pajamas, he sat on the bed supported by cushions and pillows. He then placed the file on his lap and unfolded it.

He read, *Shukno Pata, by Niranjan Sarkar.*

Time ticked by and he inched on. The pages unleashed a world unknown.

It told him the story of a very ordinary drink, served in a very unceremonial manner in every average Indian home, irrespective of occasion or emotion. Tea.

Words drew him into the pensive of his father's mind; into the struggling life of the tea-garden laborers.

Laboriously drafted, extensively researched, it depicted the socio-cultural lives of the garden dwellers across India, detailing how a leaf that had its origin in China, was introduced by the British into India, had affected the lives of a large section of population who work in there. How the breath-taking, lush- green tea gardens, undulating over acres of land on the slopes and foothills; pristine, serene, mesmerizing to the eye of every passerby, holds at its roots, the poverty-stricken, ignorant, painfully deprived lives of those, whose hard-work brings colour to the cup; whose sweat smells in its aroma; whose tears bestows the taste that makes it the best beverage served all over the world.

It exposed a million dollar industry that had its foundation smeared with the highest rate of female and child mortality; of domestic violence; of pitiful condition of human thrown to destitute due to negligence, both from the society and the concerned authorities; who take pride in a cup of hot tea.

Every page turning into the next, pinned him down even more. The document contained paper cuttings of various articles, written at different times, pictures, photographs, names, addresses, contact numbers et cetra.

Captivated, Shubham didn't see the daylight streaming in through the windows, illuminating the room. He didn't either notice that his cell phone had been buzzing continuously for some time.

When ultimately, he was on the last sentence of the document, that its ringing pierced into his skull to reach his grey cells. He picked it up mechanically.

'Where are you Shubham?'

The wail was not only loud but desperate. It jolted him inside out.

'You should be in the office by now!' The yelling continued.

'What office?'

Still roaming amongst the stubby tea shrubs, he asked unmindfully.

'Shyamal here sir. You are to sign an agreement regarding the sale of your house.'

The spectacular pictures of ravishing tea gardens fell to fragments by the harsh blow of reality.

It was twenty past nine. He should be in the property dealer's office. The buyer would be reaching any moment. He needed to wash, change and run.

Instead, he remained crucified on to the bed; immobile, numb; his eyes staring the lines written on the page.

He had been waiting for that day; to shed off the burden his father had left behind; to have the money to start anew. He should be happy; his plan had materialized smoothly.

But he wasn't.

An unidentified force, an unseen knot held him tied to the bed; as though paralyzed, he couldn't move his limbs to propagate himself. Like a rock on his chest, the weight was crushing him. He felt as if something very important, very innate, something belonging to his own body was to be cut off; he felt as though being emasculated.

Closing his eyes, he focused on the cause of his anxiety. His house. The magnificent, red-brick house named Niranjan Nibas.

Shubham disintegrated into a flood of tears; hot lava flowing out of his heart moistening his cold skin and dry lips before falling on to make big blotches on the finely inked lines.

Like a revelation, realization washed over him draining out every doubt, every falsehood, every bit of enigma, he had been clinging on to for all these years.

He wanted to sell his house not just for money.

He had hated his father for not being a considerate husband and an efficient father. He had held him responsible for his mother's death; for losing out on Monalisa and Mereline. Even wished him dead. But his grudge against his father didn't die with his death. He still kept blaming him for his failures, his shortcomings. Even the house which was a part of his father's identity, was not spared. Need for money was merely a pretext, a cover to hide his malicious plan to erase Niranjan Sarkar off the land; from the place where he had created himself. To make him non-existent; kill him permanently.

And in his blind race to punish his father, he had wounded himself beyond endurance.

Odium and jealousy, were the diseases he had been a patient to, that didn't let him see anything with clarity. He shut his eyes in acceptance. His immature mind could not fathom the complicacies of an adult relationship and judged his father as guilty; his incompetent self could not digest to be recognized by his father's fame and grew envious of him. All his pain that he had been suffering, was self-incurred.

He had conveniently chosen his father as his scapegoat to escape the challenges of his life; to be an excuse for his disruptive self.

Monalisa and Mereline, both were a part of the same act.

Monalisa was nothing more than a teenage fascination that he had used to insult and molest his father's respect to satisfy his wild hunger; and Mereline was like a trophy he liked to flaunt as a payback for Monalisa; a means to get square and settle the score with him.

His emotions and decisions, negative or positive, then and now, always had been guided by no one other than his father; the man who had died in the isolation of a small cabin waiting for him, missing him.

'I miss you too, Baba!'

A cry erupted shattering the silence of the room.

'I was a fool not to have accepted it! Not to have seen that I am nothing without you!'

He kept screaming like a mad man, letting out all that had been held-up within him.

Man can live either in love or in hatred. He had spent an eternity hating his father. Never had he provided him with a chance to close up, bridge the gap and discern the truth. From the trough of his substandard perception of his father's character to the peak of glory, Prokash Mitra had attributed to him, his father could have been anybody, but prejudiced, he chose never to evaluate the real Niranjan Sarkar. Never had really tried to know him nor would he be able to do it ever now. And, the truth was flushing out, draining out the debris from within. He kept crying, wishing if only he could rewind the time, he could at least try to correct the mistakes;

could at least say a proper 'goodbye' to them. He kept waiting for his mother who never came out of her room; he had rushed to the hospital but his father had given in by then, rendering their farewell incomplete; leaving him disgruntled.

Tears continued flowing out, cleansing him, rejuvenating him.

He began feeling light. The rock weathered and the pebbles, washed away.

Opening his eyes, he closed the file and dropped it aside.

Like a dew drop jiggling on the Colocasia leaf; like a young nestling, spreading its tiny wings to take its first leap, he felt being born again.

Like a new, tender tea-leaf, unfolding to the Sun; unaware of its fate yet fearless, ready to take in the hardships of life; ready to be plucked, wilted, macerated, sweltered, dried and cured; he felt strong, ready to be tested and to fail; only to rise again and become a name.

His father had written,

'chasing and accomplishing dreams makes one feel worthy, but while doing so, we should never forget who we are. It makes us the man we want to be; only then can we live fearlessly.'

The words fell right in their blocks solving the puzzle.

Sniffing hard, wiping the slimy mucous with the sleeves of his shirt, taking few deep breaths to fill his constricted lungs with air, he walked over to the window and pushed it open to let warm rays in, to illuminate his room, his mind.

He knew who he was, had known it all along. In fact, he was born with it. His father wasn't the rust, decaying his life but his roots. Shubham Sarkar was but a part, a canopy of Niranjan Sarkar.

His cell buzzed again.

'Shubham....where are you?'

'Shyamal....I cannot come. Actually....I am not selling the house anymore.'

That was something, his agent wasn't able to digest easily. For the breach, he was penalized and asked to pay a hefty compensation, which Shubham agreed to without much debate.

Next, he pulled out a card from his purse and dialed a number. It was answered instantly.

'Shubham. I was beginning to worry.'

'Prokash uncle. There is just one thing to worry. How soon can we get started?'

The man at the other end yelled in joy. Shubham smiled too. Life definitely was bountiful. We only require to be approving to enjoy it.

'Uncle, it is Baba's last project. It has to be done his way.'

'Son, if I had to betray Niranjan, I could have done it long ago. Don't worry. We'll bring him to life!'

The smile on his face broadened.

Disconnecting, he dialed another number. There was one more score to settle.

'Hello. This is Shubham Sarkar. Am I talking to Mr. Dasgupta?'

Chapter 13

'Ma, will you tell Baba?'
        'You tell me...what should I do?'
Mrs. Chatterjee looked up at him. It was four days since his rendezvous with the law. He was repentant and scared. He had promised her assuring that such a situation would not arise again. She was not sure if she should take his words but she knew, she had to trust him; provide him with a second chance to prove himself; to see if he actually meant his words, before taking any stern measure.

Mr. Chatterjee had returned the night before. The presence of his father was causing her son to shiver.

As an acquiescent wife and a conscientious mother, she found it obliging to let her husband and the guardian, know about the developments during his absence. However, her past experiences warned her against any such disclosure.

It was a complex situation. If she kept the secret and Joy eased away and grew careless, she would lose not just her position but her faith in her son as well, weakening the cord of umbilicus. And if she updated her husband of his actions, he would not spare his son and that would widen the crater between them.

The days were short and evening approached earlier than wished. Her brain had been ricocheting; analyzing the pros and the cons of the two options she had.

The door of the house was drawn apart at around six in the evening and she heard her husband's footsteps marching up the stairs. Gathering courage, she counted the steps up with a tray loaded with snacks of his liking, hoping to put across the issue with utmost care and sensitivity so as to make him understand her perception. Joy needed to be handled wisely.

'Close the door.'

Mr. Chatterjee ordered the moment she entered the bedroom. He was raw, she could sense. Placing the tray on the writing table by the wall, she walked back to close the door deciding to defer the idea for the time being. No sooner had she pushed the door shut, she realized him to be standing close, on her back. She turned.

In a second, he grabbed both her hands in a strong grip and twisted them backwards, pulling her to paste on him. She was surprised by his aggression; his malevolent dark eyes, threateningly boring into hers. Tightening his clutch, he pushed her pinning on to the door, fixing her with the weight of his gigantic body.

'What was he doing in my house?' He hissed into her ears.

The latch on the door was cutting into her back, causing intolerable pain. Her fingers were growing numb in his firm hold; her brain trying to register the gist of the assault.

'Did you invite him?'

'You are hurting me!'

'Answer me!'

He bellowed tearing her ears; his nails and the edge of the latch, mercilessly tearing into her flesh.

'I have no idea what you are talking about?'

'Lie!'

He screamed banging her on the door. She cried out in pain.

'Arundhati saw him sneaking out of the house in the middle of the night!' His high pitched voice reverberating her drums, deafening her. 'Why was he here? To celebrate the new year with you!'

A lightening realization of the matter jammed all her senses. Her brain locked; her pain disapparated by the horrendous blow.

'You slut! How much did you offer him?'

Burns incurred by his words were more scorching than his force, smoldering her to the core.

'I was worried about Avni. How on earth I was to imagine that this old bitch would be oozing in his love!'

He twisted her wrist, stimulating her sensory nerves to action, generating excruciating pain. She began wriggling to get free.

'Please. Stop!'

She whispered. She wasn't able to endure his slanders. She had hacked Shubham out of her life to uphold the dignity of her marriage; to maintain his respect.

'Why should I stop when you didn't stop before slurring my name. Every damn house is feasting on the stories of Mr. Chatterjee's wife and her lover! Your illicit liaison with that scoundrel is what people are spitting on my face!'

'No! Don't you trust me?'

'How can I? I should have understood when I saw you both that day in that filthy store! How long has this been going on?'

In spite of the cold air, they both were wet, sweating from the heat fuming out of their mind and body.

'Stop insulting me!'

She shouted and jerked a violent push out to him, misbalancing him and made one of her hand to slip out of his grip. She didn't waste time but pulled out her other hand. Planting both her hands on his chest and with all her might, she shoved him aside and ran out of his clutch.

'Do you think you have an honor that I need to respect?' He roared. 'You are no better than those who walk the streets selling themselves. At least...they do that to earn their bread! What is it that I didn't give you....that you went begging to him?'

'And you abuse me after all that I have done for you?' She retorted. 'After standing beside you at every point..... after all those compromises....all these years.....you believe Arundhati's words!'

'Compromise? You are my biggest compromise!' He growled. 'If it wasn't for my obstinate mother.....you wouldn't have been here at the first place!'

Mrs. Chatterjee stared at her husband with wide eyes, open mouth and a blank face. His eyes were spilling hatred, she had never seen before.

'If it wasn't for that stupid sister of yours...I would have been a very happy man! Who asked her to get tangled with that lustful...shameless...selfish friend of hers and....kill herself out of guilt!'

Tears poured out of her eyes. The man who stood there screaming like a lunatic had let out a secret she had no intelligence about.

He...was in love with her sister!.....Still!

His ferociously dark eyes had gone damp at the mention of her; his words smeared with love even when uttered in anger as swear.

She might have replaced Kakoli in his life but not in his heart. No wonder, he never took any notice of her; never appreciated her.

All those years of her devotion; all those years of services, were reduced to zilch; zero. She was a compromise; a burden, a nobody.

'Didi didn't die...because of guilt. She killed herself because she couldn't bear to see you marry someone else. She had cried the whole night before.'

The wrestling room dropped to rest. Mr. Chatterjee sank into his rocking chair by the bed; calm and quiet.

Mrs. Chatterjee too settled by the edge of her bed. She didn't know what her husband was thinking but she was definite, his thoughts were even remotely not relating to her. He seemed to be lost, unaware of her existence, inconsiderate of his abrasive ill-treatment on her.

She examined her hands. They were swollen, bruised and paining. But it was no equivalent to the ache, her heart was living through. She had toiled twenty-five years of her life for absolutely nothing. The man who was supposed to be a part of her body, her soul had never considered her to be a part of him.

Love had not been on her cards, she had known. But what tortured her more was that, she had been unsuccessful in evoking even meager sense of sympathy in him whose heart was not infertile but green in love for her sister, even after all those years of her death.

Mrs. Chatterjee, her title sounded meaningless. Her only identity, wiped out. She went empty, drained-out; support-less like a vine ripped from its twigs.

The whole universe, with its stars, planets, comets, every entity had an identity, a purpose, except for her. She felt like a speck of dust, insignificant; useless; aimless.

She took few deep breaths, collected her feeble self and stood up. At the threshold of her room, at the door, she turned to look at her husband. He was rocking on his chair; his face on the other side. She was unable to see.

She pulled the door and stepped out.

'I know I am not qualified but I will try my best. Please tell your friend to be a little patient.'

'Don't worry. He is well aware about your limitations and he is ok with it. He knows how to use you. So have faith in yourself.'

'Thank you for believing in me.'

Yash forced an awkward smile at her. She smiled back at him in gratitude and took his leave. She knew she had startled him by landing at his office that day.

Stepping under the Sun, she let the rays wash over her, energizing her; waking her up from her slumber. A long sleep that had paralyzed her flesh; anesthetized her brain, rendering her incapable of independent thinking. She realized, she was left with just one choice if she was to survive. To re-search and re-define herself; to find a purpose, a use of her.

*   *   *

.....A book that is very different from the regular ones where emotions are inked in lines to cover the emptiness of white sheets; one that takes birth, breathes, lives and dies. Not one, where stories lay scattered in words but are lived in moments. Not one, which makes its readers laugh or lament at the pleasure or plight of the created characters but one, that shoulders the burden of real agony and rejoices the ecstasy of true happiness. One that cannot be finished in a day's time or a month or a year but requires a life's time to complete-- sometimes even beyond. One, where a page or a chapter cannot be skipped or turned back.

A book where time turns the pages, changes the chapters; one after the other in perfect chronology. And with every turning page, with every changing chapter, personalities unfolds; layer by layer, revealing such surprising qualities of one's own character, the existence of which was neither ever known nor expected.

The most unpredictable; the most unbelievable book ever written---Man.

Folding back the magazine, Shubham rolled it up, admiring the credentials of her words.

When Yash had informed him that she had started to work, he felt a petite waft of relief. She had at least valued his request, but it didn't completely rinse him off the pain she had infused him into. The wound was still tender.

At the crux of his heart, he couldn't deny that she was in a way responsible for the presently persisting content in him; for the passion; for his new outlook towards life. Yet, he couldn't get over their last raw.

Despite his busy schedule, his heart still ached when the Sun set by the shores of the mighty Brahmaputra. His dreams still held her amidst the purple sky and blue grass with the rays brushing her hair; her mesmerizing densely lashed doe eyes capturing most of his days.

Against all odds, his doubts clarified. He loved her; such love, that he had never lived before. One that he could neither achieve, nor could shed off; the most surprising aspect of his character to unfold.

Nonetheless, he kept his promise. He had stayed in touch with her through her articles. Considering all his emotions, he still couldn't help but adored reading her.

'Son, let's go. The caravan is ready.'

Prokash Mitra came running, hauling everyone to move to the vehicle. Shubham knew why his mentor was fidgety. They were in the beautiful state of Assam, working on his father's film, *Shukno Pata*, amongst its lavish tea gardens.

Mist had veiled most of the days and they were yet to cover few of the most breathtaking gardens. Time was running out, so was money and Mitra was determined to finish it on schedule, within the budget without compromising the quality; a trademark of Niranjan Sarkar.

Throwing away the shawl, hoisting his backpack, he placed the magazine on the table and moved ahead.

It was time for him to be the man he wished to become.

Printed in the United States
By Bookmasters